LIBRARIES NI
WITHDRAWN FROM STOCK

To Patrick, Eoghan, Claire and Sinéad.

With love.

Author's Note

Readers of *The Accidental Wife* will recognise many of the characters who inhabit the pages of *Full of Grace*. I never imagined that the stories of quiet, ordinary people, living ordinary lives in an extraordinary time and place would strike such a chord with readers across the globe and, of course, with those of us who navigated the years of the Troubles in the north of Ireland. As is also true of *The Accidental Wife*, the people and the stories in *Full of Grace* are works of fiction.

But I must mention the story '1972'. I was born in 1972, 'the worst year' of the Troubles, and have always wondered how it might have felt to bring new life into the world at that time. The historical figures in the story, both those who thrust themselves into the political limelight, and those who were injured, killed and traumatised by events beyond their control, find a record in this story. I hope I have done them justice.

LIBRARY
WITHDRAWN

Contents

Full of Grace

:::::

'Say the Hail Mary.'

'What?'

'Say the Hail Mary, wee lad. We're all ears.'

Shit. How am I going to get out of this one?

There are three of them and only one of you.

The boys have stepped out of the sweet-scented cow-parsley verge and you've had to pull hard on the brakes, wrenching the front wheel round in a dusty arc to avoid crashing into them. They're all wearing shiny new black boots. No one you know can afford boots like that.

Shit.

They are looking for trouble. They haven't even had the wit to cover their faces. You can see them clearly but you've never clapped eyes on them before. You should have pedalled faster and made them decide whether baiting you was worth the pain of getting run over.

A stick hangs casually from each boy's right hand and you look to the sticks for help. They might give you a clue. Hurleys would tell you one thing, and you could give them the answer they want and be home and safe in ten minutes. Boys holding hockey sticks or cricket bats would mean something different, more dangerous; still, there's a chance you could get away unbruised. But these boyos heft two blackthorns and an ashplant. They have not nailed their colours to the mast. They're not just looking for trouble, they're looking for sport as well. They're going to make you guess what answer they want.

'Say the Hail Mary, wee lad. We're awful religious, and we just love to hear a wee fella saying his prayers.'

You think hard and fast. You could offer to say the Pater Noster instead. You know it in English, and don't both Prods and Catholics say the Our Father?

But wait. There's something odd about the Proddy Our Father, something different about it. They say 'which art in heaven', not 'who art in heaven', don't they? This makes them godless heathens, according to Father Martin's catechism class. It's a strange thing to fight to the death over, but they'll notice if you say the wrong one. The Our Father isn't going to help.

Then you remember your da, ranting and raving last week in the milking parlour. 'Thon hoors over at McGeady's are after selling the six-acre paddock.'

'Our six-acre paddock?' your older brother Alo had asked.

'Well, obviously it's not ours if they're after selling it, ya gom.'

'But we graze it. We always graze it.'

'Well, we'll not be grazing it any more, for it's sold. I seen them coming out of McGeady's and spitting on their hands to seal the deal. Why McGeady couldn't have come to me first, or had the bloody thing to auction like an honest man, I'll never know.'

Your da had taken a deep breath and gobbed out a thick wedge of tobacco-phlegm near the toe of your welly.

'Maybe the new owner will let us graze it,' you'd chipped in.

'Not a chance, not a chance in hell. He's as Orange as a Jaffa.'

You've never seen a real orange, or a banana either, even though the war has been over this seven years past. But it wasn't the time to draw attention to irrelevancies.

'How do you know he's a Prod, Daddy? What's his name?'

'I don't need to know a man's name to know his type.' Your father's huge white eyebrows nearly joined in the middle with the scowl. 'I'm living in Tyrone all my life – long enough to know what a man is by looking at his face.'

You study the faces of the three boys in the lane. They are all older than you and have more than a passing resemblance to each other. There's a bigger age gap between oldest and youngest than you'd normally find in a group of friends out to start a row. All in new boots. All in waistcoats. They are brothers, surely. These must be the sons of the new owner of the six-acre paddock. And that means they are Protestants.

Relief floods through you and you give your body a sudden shake as you sense how close your bladder has come to emptying itself. Now you know the answer to their unspoken question.

'I'll not say the Hail Mary.' You smile at the boys and try to look calm, though your heart's fit to burst with your own cleverness. 'What would I be doing, spouting that oul' papish nonsense? Get out of the road now, lads, and I'll be away on home.'

You grip the handlebars and lift your right leg to swing it over the crossbar and away when the middle boy's fist hits you a right puck in the gob. It hurts like hell, but the shock of crashing onto the paved road with the old Triumph keeling over on top of you is worse.

'Bloody Prod,' screams the oldest boy, all bared teeth and flaring nostrils like a nappy pony. 'You dirty Orange bastard. *Oul' papish nonsense*? You'll say a Hail Mary before you leave this place or you'll go home in a box.'

'What?'

'What? I'll tell you what. I'm Joseph Mary Devlin. This here's Francis Xavier Devlin, and babyface over there is Peter. Don't forget us, boy, and do yer best to stay clear of us, for we're here to stay and we're getting our retaliation in first, if you know what I mean.'

Francis Xavier steps forward and says slow and calm, 'I'll help you. Just listen carefully, make no mistakes and we'll all be on our way. No need for any oul' bother.' He takes a deep breath and raises his right arm. You flinch, but he laughs and touches his fingers to his forehead. 'In the name of the Father, and of the Son and of the Holy Ghost.'

Joseph Mary gives you a dunt with his shiny new boot. 'Come on, even Prods know how to bless themselves, don't they?'

You haven't lived as long as your father. You didn't see what he said he could see in a man's face. You believed in the lies of the shiny new boots and the fancy waistcoats. See where that's got you! What will you do now? Continue the pretence, say the prayer, cycle home and prepare to explain away your fat lip? But what if Peter Devlin turns up at the schoolhouse on Monday morning with his books under his arm? Then he'll know you were lying, denying the faith. Then what? You make a decision.

'Lads, sure I was only messing with you. I was only acting the oul' cod.'

You pull yourself up off the road and lean the bike into the lee of a whitethorn bush in full flower, drinking in the sweetness and purity of the white blossoms before you turn back to the boys.

You rummage in your pocket and pull out your everyday rosary, the brown beads rubbed almost black.

'Sure I was only acting the lig, lads.' You hold out your right hand towards Joseph Mary and adopt a stiff and formal manner. 'It's a pleasure to meet you. I'm Anthony O'Donovan, and I've been saying the Hail Mary since before I had teeth. English, Irish or Latin – you choose. Sure I'm a fuckin' altar boy in Drumaleish church. *Ora pro nobis* and all that.'

'You fuckin' weasel.'

'Seriously, I was just letting on I was a Prod. It was a joke.'

'Me arse it was a joke. You're a disgrace to the nation, denying your faith. Was it for this that Connolly and Pearse were taken out and shot?'

'Well, you know as well as I do that James Connolly didn't give a tinker's curse about the Catholic Church and – '

All three Devlins jump on you. Joseph Mary and Francis Xavier have decent right hooks on them; Peter is holding you by the legs. You all come crashing down to the road in a hail of fists and boots and hair and nails.

How many mistakes can one fuckin' eejit make in a day? What the fuck was I doing, trying to give these three oafs a history lesson? He's named after Joseph Mary Plunkett, for God's sake.

'Don't be scrabbing like a wee girl,' Francis Xavier shouts as you rake your nails down his face, 'Jesus, can't you fight like a man?'

'Against three of you yella hallions?' you manage to say between the gasps and the whoops and the punches. One boy is a small enough target for six flying fists. 'You'd know plenty about fighting like men!'

Now Joseph Mary has your left arm up tight behind your back and you can feel your own close-cropped hair bristling against the knuckles of your left hand. You swear the sinews are going to give.

'Stop it. For Christ's sake stop it. You've had your fun.' And then, you say it. The words spill out of your mouth – your brain isn't involved – the words you will spend the rest of your life in atonement for. The words whose undeniable truth you will deny for the rest of your life.

'This is a load of shit. You don't even believe it yourself, no more than I do. There's no Catholic and no Protestant, on earth or in heaven, because every eejit knows there's no such thing as God. Say yer prayers, kneel down for yer ma, fill the holy water font at the front door for fear the priest will find it dry if he visits. But sure youse know as well as I do that it's all a load of shit.'

Peter lets go of your legs and jumps to his feet. Francis Xavier drops his fists and looks at you like you're a bad smell. Joseph Mary lets go of your arm, then hawks up and spits straight in your face.

You try to wipe the slabber away with your left hand, but your shoulder screams with pain and you have to use your right hand, which leaves you totally defenceless. No need to worry, for the Devlin brothers never strike you again as long as they live.

At last Peter speaks.

'We're sorry, alright? We're sorry. We just wanted to be sure the word got around that we're hard fellas and then people would leave us alone.'

Francis Xavier nods. 'It's true. We never meant any real harm. Why didn't you just say the bloody Hail Mary and that would have been the end of it?'

'Come on,' says Joseph Mary, dropping to his knees in the dust of the road and waving to his brothers to do the same. 'Come on, Anthony. We're sorry. We never should have pushed you so hard. We'll all say it together.'

'It's true – it's all true,' you say. You turn to the bike and heave it out of the hedge with your good hand. 'It's true and you know it. It's 1952, for God's sake. We're not peasants in the Dark Ages. We have the wireless and the Pathé news.'

They stare at you, blank as fresh slates.

'Do youse really think there's a god that lets the Germans shovel millions of people into ovens? Do youse think our Blessed Mother in heaven looks down at Russian soldiers chasing wee holy nuns with fixed bayonets, and doesn't get her magic, all-powerful son to blast them to kingdom come?'

You straddle the bike and balance on one shaking leg, your other foot on a pedal. 'Because the kingdom's not coming. That's why.'

'Stop it, Anthony. Come on, we said we're sorry. There's no call for this. We're sorry we acted the maggot. We'll say it with you. Hail Mary …'

'Say the Hail Mary,' echoes Peter.

'Come on. Say it. Say a fuckin' Hail Mary. We're really sorry. We only wanted to give someone local a few slaps to set the tone, not steal the immortal soul out of your body.'

As you wobble away from them you hear their plaintive cries. 'We'll say it for you. Hail Mary, full of grace, the Lord is with thee …'

::::::

'Hail Mary … Say the Hail Mary.'

'Just the one is it? Say *one* Hail Mary?'

'Hmm?'

'Just the one Hail Mary?'

'What?'

You sit up with a start and come back from miles away and decades ago.

'Just the one Hail Mary is it, Father O'Donovan? I mean, I done my Act of Contrition alright, but I never told you my sins.'

'Oh, sorry.'

You pull at your collar and try to get the top open, but wrestling with a clerical collar in the dark is no easy matter. Thank God – figure of speech – you're in the traditional box with a decent mesh between you and the penitent, not one of those hateful bright 'reconciliation rooms'.

'What age are you, my child?' you ask.

'Will we start again then, Father?'

'Yes, go on.'

'Forgive me Father, for I have sinned – '

'I doubt that.'

'What?'

'What age did you say you were?'

'I'm nine and a half, Father.'

'You haven't sinned, my child. You're just a little boy who sometimes acts the eejit and puts his poor mother astray in the head. I'd say that's about right, isn't it?'

'Well, I told you the same ones last time and you never said I hadn't sinned.'

'Let me guess – said a bad word, were disrespectful to your mother, didn't clean your room?'

'Yes.'

'Mrs Rafferty always chooses the same list of sins, and by the time her pupils are old enough to actually commit any real ones, I'm the last person they'd come to for help.' You sigh. 'Do you understand?'

'No, Father O'Donovan.'

'Alright. Let's get on with it. Your sins are forgiven. Go and sin no more.'

'And the Hail Mary?'

'What?'

'Just the one is it, like?'

'Yes. No – wait.'

The child pauses, mid crouch, half risen, hand already on the door. God knows – turn of phrase – what the hell he thinks is going on.

'Say one Hail Mary for your penance.' You hear the child sigh and then you add, 'and say one for me.'

The Gospel According to Luke

:::::

'What useless carn is responsible for this?'

Your father's furious bellow echoes around the farmyard and you flinch as though struck. The question requires no answer. No matter what small crime has been perpetrated, which chore left undone, it will be your fault, while your father and your older brother, Aloysius, shake their heads or, disbelieving, hawk a gob of snot onto the ground beside your boots.

'What did I do to be cursed with such a useless shower of bastards?' your father's litany continues, as you drag yourself out from the pighouse, where you have been shaking down a new straw bed for the soon-to-be-born litter, and cross the yard to the lambing pens.

Pushing open the door, you wait for your eyes to adjust to the cool dimness inside and mentally run through a list of tasks completed. Have you tossed the bedding properly? You know you have. And the hay – you had coughed and spluttered as you winnowed out the dust that is so injurious to the newborn lambs before bringing it inside to replenish the mangers. Have you checked each bucket of water is full and clean? All present and correct. You can't think how you might have failed this morning – redding out the lambing shed is the easiest job of all, which is why you are entrusted with it.

From your father's left hand an hours-old lamb dangles, hind hooves tiny in the man's giant gnarled fist while the front hooves graze the floor of the shed. Molly, the blue roan crossbred, is blaring and roaring from her pen, striking the ground with her hard front foot, stretching and craning her neck above the top rail, demanding the return of her lamb. You have never told your father or your brother that the ewe is called Molly, or that you have already chosen 'Zebra' for the lamb for the unusual pattern of stripes across his withers. The great Luke O'Donovan and his eldest son, Alo, have no time for such sissy, pansified notions.

Zebra is dead. Of that there is no doubt. The black protruding tongue and the popping, bulging eyes could not belong to a living being.

'This is your doing.'

'I don't think so, Daddy. He was perfect when I left him – less than an hour ago, I'd say.'

Your father throws the carcass at your feet. 'Pick it up.'

He knows you hate dead things, that you vomited in the hen house the morning after the fox's visit, even dread the task of opening the rat traps.

'Yes, Daddy.'

Holding your breath you lift the lamb from the ground, fighting back hot tears and a lump in your throat that will make your voice shake and earn you a cuff round the back of the head. The animal is still warm and dry and well cleaned of its birth slime – Molly has always taken motherhood seriously. She will not have lain down upon her lamb, like a new-delivered hogget sometimes will, nor will she have crushed him against the wall, knocked him into the water bucket or employed any of the other means by which sheep strive to die or to kill each other.

Wrapped tightly around the lamb's neck is the length of blue rope that you carried into the lambing shed that morning, the rope that secures the door at night against the foxes and the crows that your father says will pluck the soft, succulent eyes from newborn lambs. You don't believe him; you don't believe that any mother would stand by and admit of such an atrocity. You can see how the lamb had twisted this way and that, each doomed struggle looping another twist in the unforgiving ligature until the tiny windpipe collapsed and the body gave up the fight.

'What do you do with the rope in the morning?'

'You hang it on the peg beside the door.'

'And yet, lo and fucking behold, the peg is empty and the lamb is dead. It's a fucking mystery, that's what it is. The rope has clean jumped off the peg and walked the length of the shed to the farthest pen. Would you say that's what's after happening?'

There is nothing to say. You brought the rope to the farthest pen. You heard the soft, happy noise of Molly in the first joyous hours of maternity and rushed, unthinking, to stroke and pet your favourite's fine new lamb. You did not pause, as constantly instructed, to hang the rope on its accustomed peg, and when, finally, you turned late to the task of filling the buckets, you lost sight of the blue rope and never gave it another thought.

'What are you?'

There is nothing to say but the truth. 'I'm sorry, Daddy. It's my fault.'

'You're a useless, fucking careless, throughother carn, that's what you are. What are you?'

'I'm a useless, careless, throughother carn.'

You are not sure if censoring your father's words is the right thing to do but he doesn't seem to notice. Your voice is surprisingly steady, but you can't look at him. The scorn and bewilderment in his stare will finish you off completely. How has your father been cursed with such a useless bastard of a son? What has he ever done to deserve it? You have heard the questions a thousand times but you are no closer to reaching an answer.

Your father reaches for the buckle of his belt and draws it open. You sigh, but it's no more than you deserve.

With the belt removed from half the loops of his trousers, your father pauses and pulls free the folding knife he wears in a scabbard always hanging within reach at his left hip. The knife is his pride and joy; a dozen razor-sharp blades, spikes, prongs, pincers and God knows what else are folded into its hollow horn handle. Alo knows that he will get the knife when your da dies – the knife and the farm to go with it – while you will live on in your childhood bed in his shadow, unless you can find a woman with a farm of her own. But why would any woman marry the most useless cur in the townland?

The knife lands at your feet in the passageway.

'Go and ask your mother for the twine and the biggest needles from the sewing kit.'

'No!' The word is out before you have time to stop it. It is almost a shout. 'No, please no, Daddy. I can't.'

'You'll clean up your own fucking mess for once.'

'Please don't make me.' You know you sound like a wee girl, and that he knows the tears are barely contained and will slip out with the next breath. 'Please, Daddy, for the love of God. Will I ask Alo to do it and I'll do his jobs? Please Daddy.'

'Do you think I'd let a hopeless wee blirt like you into the dairy when I can't even trust you to bed down a few sheep?'

'Please, Daddy. I can't. You know I can't.'

Your father turns on his heel and strides out to the yard. In the sudden silence of the lambing shed the ping of milk hitting the sides of a galvanised bucket can be clearly heard as Alo skilfully wrings the cows' long teats in the dairy next door. Everything comes easily to Alo.

As you bend to pick up the knife, Molly starts a frantic bleating and bawling again and you know that what is to be done must be done straight away, before she loses interest.

:::::

Your mother shakes her head and the blood runs from her cheeks when you explain about the twine and the needles.

'Jesus, Mary and Joseph, is yer father out of his tiny mind? Asking you to do that when it's clear as day that yer not made of farming stuff? Sit down by the stove there for a minute, son, and I'll go out to him.' She takes off her apron and pushes her arms into the sleeves of her coat.

'No, Mammy, leave it. And leave him be. I can do it. Just give me the needles.'

'You won't be able to do it, a wee soft fella like you. Let me talk to him.'

You shake your head. Your mother won't rest until she has you stuck in Belfast in the diocesan seminary or, even better, at St Patrick's in Maynooth, where they get *a better class of young fella altogether.* She already has you in your alb and robes, serving old Father Smith on the altar each Sunday, and talks of buying you a Latin primer and finding the money to send you to a secondary school. If she goes out to the dairy and rescues you from this horror, you will owe her more than you already do, and saying no to the seminary and breaking your mother's heart will be harder than ever.

You don't want to live on the farm forever, the boy to Alo's man, but anything is better than the seminary.

::::::

You are wearing thin cotton gloves to keep your human smell from polluting the dead lamb, whose scent must already be fading.

Zebra is lying on his back in a cradle of straw, legs splayed, already stiffening. The long string of his navel has not yet started to shrivel. He had been born sometime between the last check of the lambing shed last night and the first check this morning, when you found him already standing and well able to operate the teat. He was not even twelve hours old.

First thing is to remove the fatal noose without shortening the rope too much: the rope is of good quality and expensive; its loss will only give your father something else to gurn about.

Your hand is shaking and there is snot in your mouth; the gloves are too big for you. You need to get a grip of yourself. If you go too deep with the knife you will cut into the flesh and the skin will not come away clean; the smell of rotting flesh will hang around for days. Too shallow and peeling the corpse will be a nightmare; it will tear and come away in patches. Let you try for once to do something properly.

Zebra's chin is firmly in your left hand now, neck stretched taut as possible. You draw the knife down his throat from chin to sternum and the skin springs apart and separates slightly. There is very little blood. You eejit, he's been dead for an hour at least now; of course there won't be much blood.

Next you circumnavigate the neck just behind the head. The knife is as sharp as a spinster's tongue and the lamb's skin is much softer than you had envisaged. When you watched this operation, through your fingers, in the past, it seemed a fearsome task of brute strength, but so far it has been easy.

Slipping your fingers under the flap of skin just below the lamb's black ear, you gently push your fingers forward, applying gentle pressure with your left hand. The sound is like the crackling of a distant bonfire as the fascia tears and peels away and your fingers slip further and further down the lamb's throat. When you rub your hand across the centre line to start peeling the other side, you feel the hard, rubbery rings of the windpipe through the warm, blood-soaked cotton gloves, and suddenly your breakfast rushes, scalding hot and acidic, into your throat. You try to swallow it, but it is too late for that now, and you fall to your knees and boke until you are just coughing and dry-retching beside the puddle of vomit.

'Right. That's it. I've had enough of this,' comes your mother's voice from outside the door of the old forge where she has lurked unseen all this time. 'You're not cut out for this life. I'm taking no more nonsense from yer da.'

You struggle to your feet and lurch to the door, leaning on the jamb, wheezing and still shaking.

'Keep your nose outta this, Ma.'

'What did you say to me?'

'I said, keep outta this. I'm nearly finished. I'll be grand. Don't you dare say a word to my daddy.'

'And don't you dare speak to me like that!'

'Why not? What are you going to do about it? This is man's business. Away back to yer kitchen.'

And it is done. The words you said wild horses would never drag from you; that your wife, God help her, would never hear from your lips. Twelve years old and that vow broken already.

Your mother's face drains, as though you had drawn the back of your hand across her mouth. Maybe a physical blow would have been less cruel. You have always been allies, you and your ma. She is the one you could trust, the one who might mutter a few words of warning, the one who might divert the seething rage of your father by taking it upon her own stooped shoulders.

Silently she turns and walks across the yard, pauses with her hand on the scullery door, looks back to speak, then shakes her head and goes into the house.

Now you must split the skin from sternum to anus, draw trembling circles with the knife around Zebra's tail and the midshank of all four legs. You must stop calling the fucking thing Zebra! It's an It. Yes, It.

Inch by inch the corpse is stripped of its hide, revealing the muscles, sinews, blood vessels and the flat, white bands of the nerves. There is a sucking sound as the skin pulls away from bubbles of fatty tissue around the haunches. The sucking sound and the grease soaking through to your fingers makes you retch again, but there is nothing left inside and the moment passes.

Finally there you have it: the corpse with its fluffy white head and little soft socks and, in between, a gory mess of muscle like the statue of St Bartholomew in the Religious Education textbook. And in your hand, inside-out, complete, flawless and clean, the flayed hide still smelling, you hope, of the lamb that was briefly Zebra.

Your father has chosen the recipient of It's skin already – the smaller of twins born to the ewe which yesterday you would have called Curly, but which now and evermore will be referred to as 'the dorset with the twisted horn'. Stitching the wriggling, struggling lamb into his new skin is a two-man job, and Alo is sent to hold him still while you stitch.

You separate the three strands of the twine and thread a strand through the eye of the needle, handing the other two strands to Alo for safekeeping. Then you grip the long, sharp needle tight in the mouth of a pair of pliers.

'You have to do it quare and tight,' Alo says.

'I know.'

'It'll have to stay on for two or three days, until the shit of its own mother's milk has run through it and the shit smells of the new mother.'

'I know.'

'Do you want me to do it for you?'

'Fuck off.'

'Ah, don't be like that. I'm serious. You houl' the lamb and I'll stitch it in and we'll tell the da you did it.'

'Fuck off, Mr fuckin' Perfect.'

He laughs then. It's a friendly enough sound – one you don't hear too often around the farm.

'Well, will ya listen to Blessed St Anthony O'Donovan. I didn't think you had it in ya.'

'You've no idea what I have in me.'

He grips the lamb and holds it so tight you think you might soon enough have another fatality on your hands, but it makes your job a lot easier and you get the knots good and tight. You've done such a careful job of the flaying that the imposter is almost perfectly covered in It's skin.

'That's a right job,' says Alo at the end when he sets the lamb back down and it struggles to its feet, seemingly none the worse for wear. 'Good man, Anthony.'

He smiles, but you don't smile back, not yet. It's going to take more than half an hour of effort for him to wipe clean his slate of all the past jibes and digs and injustices. But maybe he's not the worst in the world after all.

'And I'll help you houl' the oul' bitch down if she needs it.'

You walk together to the lambing shed and he sets the imposter down in the pen with the bereaved ewe. The two lambs were born within hours of each other and the trick should work, even if the ewe has to be hog-tied and shackled for the first two days. And if she must be, then you will do it yourself; you'll ask no man for help.

'She's taking to it,' he says as you watch the ewe sniffing the lamb from head to toe and dunting it curiously with her muzzle as if to say *where the hell have you been? I've been worried sick.*

You hold your breath because, although you are a man now, you would rather not have to hog-tie the ewe.

'He's got it, the cheeky wee blirt! Not in the pen with her five minutes and he's on the teat already. Good work, Anthony.'

The lamb's tail is shaking in an ecstasy of greed, and the ewe is nuzzling his arse and shifting her hind legs to make his life easier. She isn't completely at ease, but she's not trying to kill him either, which you have seen them try to do many's the time before.

Alo punches you on the shoulder and although it hurts, it's a good kind of pain.

'Come on in, ya big sissy, and we'll tell the da the job's a good un.'

:::::

Your mother catches your eye later, after the rosary, and drags you out to the scullery.

'Don't you dare ever speak to me like that again or I'll tell your father to redden yer arse.'

You stick your thumb into your belt where your knife would hang, if you had a knife.

'When I was a child I thought as a child but when I became a man I put away childish things. For now we see in a glass, darkly, but then all will be clear.'

'I wish to God you would stay away from the Old Testament, Anthony. It's not a good idea to read the Old Testament without a priest to guide you.'

'You're mistaken, Ma. That's from the Gospel According to Luke.'

'Are you sure?'

You look through the open door to where your da is sprawled beside the stove, his socks sending up wisps of vapour like the mist that rose into the cool morning air as you slid your hands beneath the lamb's warm skin.

'I'm pretty sure,' you lie.

Buachallain Buí

::::::

Tug and twist. Tug and twist. Down on your hunkers. Pull away the blades of coarse meadow grass from the thick red stems of the ragwort. Grass pulls up hard, and the job is hard enough already. A drop of sweat falls from your forehead into your eye, blinding and stinging. You let go of the ragwort stalks and dash the tears away, rub your sleeve across your brow.

Gather the stalks again, strong thumb of the right hand seeking the bend of the stem as it curves off and becomes root. Hands between your feet, arms between your hunkered knees. And pull and twist. And rock and rock and rock your weight gently, left and right and backwards. Left and right and backwards, and the thumb in its yellow pigskin glove following the many-fingered root down into the soil.

Crunch and crunch, and easing up into the daylight the snaking white root, obscene pale ghost of the sturdy red stem above. You try not to fall over, not to make a glipe of yourself in front of Alo, at the pop and sudden release of the buachallain buí, the yellow boy, the deadly poisonous ragwort, as it lets go its grasp on the land.

Five years now this patch of land, this once fine paddock next to your father's boundary fence, has been lying sinfully fallow, untamed, ungrazed, as the heirs and hopefuls gathered round the lawyer's table and fought over the meaning of a comma, the direction of a dash, the home-wrought will of Patsy McGonagall, a man too mean to pay the lawyer his due – or one who wanted to make a fuss from beyond the grave, your mother says, a sure-fire way to keep his memory alive among the nieces and nephews far away in London.

Five years the buachallain buí has been establishing a hold deep into the four acres of McGonagall's land and sending intruders to colonise your father's pristine, well-weeded grasslands.

'One year's seeding means seven years' weeding,' your father says, but sighs in despair when you ask if that means you will be weeding this paddock for the next thirty-five years. 'Take out the whole of each root,' he warns. 'Every plant that snaps off in yer fist will be back to taunt you in six weeks' time.' He turns away and goes back to the real work of the yard. 'Surely to God even you can manage that,' he mutters.

The deeds of the new paddock are sitting on the desk in your father's room beside the calendar and the family Bible. Field by field, parcel by parcel, the farm is expanding. Neighbouring men shake their heads when they enter the auction room and see Luke O'Donovan already ensconced. They make their bids but know they will lose. Your father has a hunger and it will not be sated as long as he walks the earth. You are still calling the yellow-streaked field 'McGonagall's', but soon, when the ragwort is gone and the docks and thistles have been beaten back into the hedgerow, your da will re-christen it.

You turn and carefully throw the uprooted plant onto the rising pile so that the full extent of the root network can be seen. Perhaps Alo will notice when next he comes to empty his crateful of weeds on the pile and cast you a kind word, as he has done sometimes since you stitched the twin lamb into his new skin. Alo need not be here but he has come regardless, his forearms as thick as your thigh, his shoulders massive under the collarless shirt. He will pull, in the half hour he has free, as much ragwort as you will pull in the yawning gap between now and dinner.

A foot away you spy another plant, eighteen inches tall, the yellow blooms already shifting to the grey of seed. Seven years, you think to yourself. In seven years you will be nineteen, a year younger than Alo is now. Alo will be married and perhaps your father will be in the early grave your mother scries for him. Old bridegrooms leave young heirs. And maybe, if your father's lust for land continues unabated, he will leave two farms.

Now that you are a man and have put away childish things, he will come to see that you should have a farm of your own.

:::::

Gather the stalks, the strong thumb of the right hand seeking the bend of the stem as it curves off and becomes root. Hands between your feet, arms between your hunkered knees. And pull and twist. And rock and rock and rock your weight gently, left and right and backwards. Left and right and backwards, and the thumb in its yellow pigskin glove following the many-fingered root down into the soil.

And *snap*! And fall backwards and stare at the broken stalks in your hands and the thick tap root, as big as a maincrop carrot, still buried in the soil. In six weeks the deadly leaves and stalks will have pushed back up through the grass and the root will be more wicked still.

Damn and blast and hell's curse it. You dash away the stupid childish tears; sure even Alo breaks the stalks sometimes. When the meadow has been mown for hay and it's been stooked and stacked and carted away to the barn, you can spend a morning picking out the weeds that you missed.

'What kind of fools are they?' your father wants to know. 'What kind of buck eejit sells a four-acre meadow not two weeks away from mowing-fit?'

'The kind of buck eejit who's spent five years and a hundred pound on a lawyer and never wants to set eyes on the bloody oul' field again,' your mother answers. 'It was the house and the home farm they were after. No one wants this paddock, four mile away, how and ever McGonagall came to hold it in the first place.'

So the grass is mowing-high and bending with the weight of its own seed, dragging at your legs as you swim through it, from one buachallain buí to the next. The paddock must be cleaned and the weeds carted away for burning soon. The hay must be made before the twelfth of July because everybody knows that the Twelfth fortnight is the hottest, driest time of the summer.

'Signs on it,' Alo says, laughing, each haymaking season. 'The sun splitting the trees for the Twelfth and snow on Saint Patrick's Day – because God's a Protestant and no mistake.'

Your father laughs while your mother hits Alo a quare flake with the tea towel round the back of the neck and blesses herself. You just sit quietly and smile at the innocence of the three of them, believing in the big bogeyman in the sky.

:::::

Gather the stalks again, strong thumb of the right hand seeking the bend of the stem as it curves off and becomes root. Hands between your feet, arms between your hunkered knees. And pull and twist. And rock and rock and rock your weight gently, left and right and backwards. Left and right and backwards, and the thumb in its yellow pigskin glove following the many-fingered root down into the soil.

You move towards the next plant and, crashing up out of the long grass, the drab brown and speckled feathers of a hen pheasant. *Kok-kok-kokking* her outrage, she flies a few hundred yards, then settles and watches you from afar. Parting the long stalks you find the scrape-nest with eight fat, near full-grown chicks silent and watchful. Of the cock there is no sign. You walk to the hedge, snap off a long branch from a weedy alder and stake it upright beside the nest. You will tell your father, and he will give the nest a wide berth when he comes through with the mowing machine.

And here comes Alo with his full crate brimming over with yellow boys. He pauses for a moment before he spills them out on the pile at the hedgerow.

'Look at this fine buachallain,' he says, holding aloft the plant of which you are most proud, the plant you carefully positioned and repositioned at the top of the pile each time. He strokes the fine detail of the root network, the long unbroken taproot and the side roots in their squirming dozens. 'Good man, yerself, Anthony,' he says. 'You'll not be long putting up a bit of muscle if you keep this up.'

You glance at your arms. 'I've seen bigger knots in black thread,' you reply, trying to keep the treacherous smile off your face.

He leans over and gently squeezes the puny bicep of your left arm, which aches and burns from the work; his fingers are like butcher's sausages. 'No bother to you, lad. In a year or two you'll be built like a brick shithouse and all the wee girls will be chasing you round the townland.'

'Much good that'll do me, and me stuck in the bloody seminary.'

'Not at all. Sure catch yerself on. We'll make a farmer out of you yet.'

Does he know something that you don't? Has your father told him he will split the land, make two farms out of one? Is the future you have barely started to hope for already a reality, discussed between the men of the house?

'D'you really think so, Alo? D'you think I have the shape of a farmer about me?'

'Of course you do. Never mind thon oul' woman's talk and tales of the collar and the parochial house. Sure you'll always have a home here with me as long as you want it. I'll be glad of the help and the company at the mart and in the milking parlour.'

He smiles and gives you a gentle dunt on the back before throwing his empty crate up on his shoulder and striding off back to the yard, to your father and the real work of the farm.

Bastards.

1972

:::::

January

Father Edward Daly creeps round a corner, eyes darting in all directions. The scant remnants of his dark hair flutter in a faint January breeze, his hat doffed in deference. The white clerical collar is easily distinguishable, but all other traces of priestly dignity have fled. It is a half-crouching, half-crawling progress he makes, his face contorted in fear and shock. Desperately clinging to some outdated notion of chivalry and decency, his trembling right hand waves a bloodstained white linen handkerchief. Behind him come four other men bearing the bleeding body of Jackie Duddy, soon to be pronounced dead.

Maeve and Eddie McGrain pore over the black-and-white images carrying the story of Bloody Sunday around the world. Maeve reaches over and grasps Eddie's hand.

'The whole world's gone mad, love,' she whispers.

'Hush, pet,' he replies, nodding at their son Mark as he builds a fortress of cushions for Teddy Mór.

Maeve and Eddie, more usually found in glorious isolation in their respective domains of kitchen and living room, sit together, gripping each other's hands tightly, stunned and silent.

February

Eddie folds the *Irish News* carefully and sets it on the table, upside down and opened at the sports section in an effort to protect his wife from the screaming headlines and images.

'Thon wee crip,' he says to her, wiping the roughened back of a hand across his eyes, exhausted from scanning the dense print, seeking enlightenment. 'Thon wee Orange carn.'

He can't hide the paper all day; Maeve will end up reading every word. William Craig, flanked by the Reverend Martin Smyth and Captain Austin Ardill, stares out from the pages. Brian Faulkner's government is circling the drain. Craig and his new organisation, Ulster Vanguard, are lurking in the long grass. What will replace Terence O'Neill's faltering programme of pathetic, piecemeal reform when Craig and his friends give Faulkner the final push and topple him from his unsteady pedestal?

Eddie takes out his scrapbook and flicks backwards. Captain – now Baron – O'Neill's words are pasted in under January 1969:

> It is frightfully hard to explain to Protestants that if you give Roman Catholics a good job and a good house they will live like Protestants because they will see neighbours with cars and television sets; they will refuse to have eighteen children. But if a Roman Catholic is jobless, and lives in the most ghastly hovel he will rear eighteen children on National Assistance. If you treat Roman Catholics with due consideration and kindness, they will live like Protestants in spite of the authoritative nature of their Church.

'Imagine,' says Eddie, sighing, 'we didn't think we could get a worse leader than that bastard O'Neill. And look at us now.'

He picks up his scissors and glue and adds today's cutting to his scrapbook.

God help those who get in our way, for we mean business, Craig had bellowed in Lisburn at the first public meeting of the Ulster Vanguard. Worshipful Master Smyth had nodded and smiled. The Orange Order would most certainly not be found wanting when the time came to *mean business*. Does Craig mean he will take Faulkner down? Or does he mean Eddie, Maeve and three-year-old Mark?

'Faulkner's a fucking numbskull,' Eddie says. 'To think he can survive after inviting Gerard Newe in to the government at Stormont.'

'He's trying to help,' says Maeve.

'For the love of Jesus, fifty years it's taken a Catholic man to be allowed into the government offices and he wasn't even fucking elected, he was invited. Craig won't stand for it. If Faulkner falls, Stormont will be prorogued.'

'Maybe we'll be better off,' says Maeve. 'What do you think, love? Maybe direct rule from Westminster won't be any worse.'

March

> We must build up the dossiers on the men and women who are a menace to this country, because one day, ladies and gentlemen, if the politicians fail, it may be our duty to liquidate the enemy.

Sixty thousand voices – the uplifted, righteous voices of sixty thousand Protestant men – cheer Craig's words and spill out of Ormeau Park.

One hundred and ninety thousand people take part in Ulster Vanguard's General Strike. Three days of chaos: power is down, water is out; business people have no option but to close their premises and shutter their windows.

Maeve and Eddie have cousins in Portadown, which is under siege. All along Portadown's 'Tunnel' the Catholic shops have no provisions, no milk for the children, no bread. Armed men, with police supervision, storm the entrance to the Tunnel, and the IRA cadre shoots back. Families flit in the night, leaving their rented homes, falling exhausted onto the sofas and floors of friends and family on the Garvaghy Road, Obins Street and Churchill Park. Those who can't leave, who have mortgages instead of rent books or who are just too stubborn, wake to find their communities altered forever, altered by the missing and the newly arrived.

Maeve McGrain prays the Sorrowful Mysteries of the rosary for their friends in other places and thanks God for her safe home in Omagh.

Eddie tries to find the newspaper, but the delivery vans have been burnt.

And that is the end of Faulkner.

April

What can be said of April?

April brings the Scarman Report into the police brutality of 1969.

April brings twenty-three IRA bombs to Northern Ireland on a warm Friday afternoon, and blows the Smithfield bus station in Belfast to smithereens.

April brings the first child to be killed by the army's new 'safe' rubber bullets. Francis Rowntree's smiling eleven-year-old face haunts Eddie's dreams.

April brings the number of deaths to a figure beyond Eddie's ability to keep track. If people don't die straight away, Eddie might miss them; they may not get their due record. Eddie's scouring of the newspapers is not infallible.

April brings the Widgery tribunal to a close.

April brings. April brings. April brings.

'Will they not stop?' asks Maeve. 'Will they not stop before the whole country is in flames?'

She places her hands protectively over her belly, already sheltering another tiny flicker of new life, and wonders what kind of world her child will enter.

May

In May, four hundred women rise up in fury and storm the Official Sinn Féin office in Derry. Young William Best, visiting friends and family in the city, has been plucked from the streets and beaten and murdered by the Official IRA. His crime?

'He's in the British Army, Maeve – the Royal Irish Rangers. What was he thinking, may God rest him, walking around Derry the way things are now? What in God's name did he expect?'

'A hangover, Eddie. For fuck's sake! You come home from the army camp in Germany on your holidays to see yer ma and yer mates and what you expect is a hangover. Not a hole in the head.'

'I know, love, I know.'

'Haven't young Irish Catholic lads been joining the British Army since God was a boy? A pay cheque, a suit of clothes and a bed of their own.'

'I know, I know.'

If Maeve lived in Derry, Eddie knows she would have been among the women storming the Official Sinn Féin office. She would have been howling her anger and screaming her fear. She would have been part of the reason why the Official IRA has kidnapped and killed its last British soldier and declared a ceasefire.

Eddie thanks God they do not live in Derry.

June

'It's over!' Maeve throws her arms around Eddie while he still has the key in the front door. She has obviously been waiting for him. 'It's over, did you hear?'

'No, love, the radio in the car is jiggered.'

'It's a truce. It's over. Starting at midnight on Monday. Thank God, it's all over.'

'Maeve, love, it's not over. There were four men shot by the army on the Glen Road at lunchtime.'

'But that was before.'

And this is after. John Hume and Paddy Devlin have been shuttling around the six counties. John Hume and Paddy Devlin have been meeting the IRA in secret. John Hume and Paddy Devlin have been meeting Willie Whitelaw, Secretary of State for Northern Ireland. John Hume and Paddy Devlin, and God knows who else behind the scenes, have been working quiet miracles.

The Irish Republican Army will suspend offensive operations from midnight, Monday, June 26, 1972, the IRA has announced, *provided that a public reciprocal response is forthcoming from the armed forces of the British Crown*.

'Now Whitelaw has to make a settlement,' says Maeve. 'Now we can all sit down together.'

'There's no way the Unionists are going to sit down with the SDLP and Sinn Féin, love. It's just not going to happen.'

'If Richard Nixon can sit down with Chairman Mao, the Prods can sit down with the IRA.'

'Mao never tried to kill Nixon, or blow his kids to kingdom come.'

'Sure, the two countries have been threatening each other with nuclear bombs this ten years or more. If Nixon can go to China, Sinn Féin can go to Stormont.'

'I hope you're right, love.'

'I know I'm right. This has been going on three years now – three years, Eddie. If they blow this chance, the women of Northern Ireland will never forgive them. How could you let this go on for another three years?'

July

Eddie likes being right. Eddie listens to the radio, reads the papers. Eddie has his finger on the pulse. Eddie likes to say 'I told you so'. But Eddie does not like being right this time.

During the thirteen days of the truce, six young men were shot, including the Orr brothers, killed by their own community for the heinous crime of choosing girlfriends from 'the other side'. In the thirteen days since the truce failed, another thirty-five have met their maker; a hundred more are in hospital. Protestant, Catholic, soldier, child, Ballymurphy, Portadown, Strabane, Derry, Crossmaglen. And Belfast. Always bloody, tortured Belfast.

Eddie brings his attention reluctantly back to his own living room.

The voice of his mother, Eibhlin, is weak and thready; old age has sucked the tone from the once sweet soprano voice that sang

Eddie to sleep more than three decades ago. 'Turning and turning in the widening gyre – '

'What the fuck are you on about?' snaps Maeve.

'Watch your mouth, Maeve. You know what I think about women cursing.'

Eddie groans quietly. The truce has collapsed in the world outside – the centre cannot hold – and inside his own home he has to referee a skirmish in the unending, unwinnable war between his mother and his wife.

'I don't give a fiddler's fuck any more,' his wife says. 'You sitting there spouting poetry when the whole world is falling apart.'

His mother opens her mouth to make things worse, so Eddie cuts across her. 'Mammy, love, Maeve's a bit out of sorts – not sleeping well and still very sick. Sure the whole situation would put years on you.'

His mother snorts and rolls her eyes. Eibhlin McGrain has carried and birthed, not the eighteen children of which Terence O'Neill has accused her, but a nice round dozen; Eddie is the youngest. Eddie has not told his mother about the days when Maeve is so ill that all she can manage is to lie on the sofa and keep young Mark from upsetting the basin of vomit. Eddie has not told his mother about the days when he comes home and eats buttered toast for his dinner. Eibhlin has lived through two world wars. Eibhlin is not one to sympathise, nor to approve of a married working man having to make toast for his dinner, then bathing and putting his only child to bed.

'Maeve, love, would you wet us a pot of tea?' he asks, and his wife gratefully escapes to the kitchen.

There are many other things that Eddie doesn't tell his mother. He hasn't told her, for instance – nor anyone else – about Maeve's trips on the bus to Belfast to buy big boxes of condoms.

Mark had been born within fifteen months of their marriage; when, seven weeks after his birth, Eddie had risked running his hand gently over his wife's nightie, Maeve had produced the rubbers.

'What the hell are them yokes?' Eddie had asked.

She had peeled one out of its protective wrapper and shown him. 'Welly boots – condoms.'

'Condoms? You've got to be fucking joking me!'

'Yes, Eddie, life's just one long joke from my point of view. I tell you what. You have the next baby, and if you don't spend nine months boking yer ring up round you, we'll go on and have the dozen babies the McGrain family seems to specialise in.'

He reached out and took the rubber from her. It was sticky and surprisingly thick. He rubbed it between his thumb and first finger and grimaced.

'Jesus, Maeve, I don't think so.'

'That's no worries, love. It was only a wee notion I had.'

The stress slipped from his shoulders and he smiled with relief. 'So we won't use them, then?'

'Not if you don't want to, Eddie love. It was just a wee idea I had.' She smiled and reached out to stroke his arm. 'I don't care if I never have sex again, and if you feel the same way, sure that's great.'

'What?'

'You can put a condom on it, or you can keep it for stirring your tea. Your choice.'

So the welly boots became a part of life, until Maeve announced it was time. She was pregnant six weeks later. Maeve is nobody's fool.

He smiles and follows her out to the kitchen, slipping an arm round her thickening waist and whispers in her ear, 'I love you.'

'It's a bloody good job, for that oul' bag would make it hard to love her son.'

'That oul' bag made me the man I am.'

'Come on, grab them biscuits.'

They are dunking their ginger snaps in their tea when the first newsflash cuts through the regular radio programming: a bomb in Belfast. Another bomb. Five more bombs. Twenty-three bombs.

Bloody Friday.

August

Eddie is haunted by the ghosts of Bloody Monday. One, two, three weeks pass and he can't shake the terror of the Claudy bombs. He can't bear to think of the four days of the week that haven't been bloodied yet.

'Eddie, love, you need to snap out of it.'

'I can't, Maeve. I can't get the wee girl out of my mind.'

Kathryn Eakin's face stares up out of his scrapbook − blonde hair and a mouth full of baby teeth, big ones, and gaps, murdered as she cleaned the plate glass window of her mother's shop on the main street of the small country town.

'One hundred people, Eddie, one hundred people killed last month. What's so special about her?'

Eddie knows but is afraid to say. Little Kathryn is special not because she is the youngest, or the most innocent, or the prettiest. She is special because she comes from Claudy, a hole-in-the-hedge, a blink-and-you'll-miss-it. Claudy is nowhere. Claudy is nothing. Claudy is not Belfast. Claudy is not the Bogside. If Merle and Billy Eakin can lose their daughter in godforsaken Claudy, Maeve and Eddie McGrain can lose their son in Omagh.

Eddie is pretty sure he is going mad.

September

Eddie has stopped counting. Eddie has stopped cutting up the *Irish News*. Eddie's scrapbook has not been added to since the 31st of July. Eddie's tally stopped in Claudy.

Maeve tells her rosary beads and makes hot soup for her husband; toast is no longer good enough. Maeve thinks she might have to call upon her mother-in-law for help. Maeve checks all the bottles in the bottom of the corner cabinet for fear that Eddie is drinking, but the bottles are as full as they were on Boxing Day, the last time she saw them. Maeve doesn't know what to do. Maeve has never not known what to do.

October

William Craig has woken Eddie from his daze. William Craig and the Ulster Vanguard are at it again. Craig has been speaking to the Conservative Monday Club in London, a few minutes' walk from the Palace of Westminster.

'That'd be right up his street,' says Eddie. 'Licking the boots and the arses of the peers of the realm. Doesn't he know those English bastards think he's scum? Doesn't he know those bastards think he's Irish?'

Maeve is delighted that William Craig has spoken at the Monday Club. Maeve doesn't care that he threatened to mobilise eighty thousand men who were *prepared to come out and shoot and kill... I am prepared to kill, and those behind me will have my full support.* Maeve doesn't care that an elected representative of a British constituency has threatened treason against the lawfully elected government. Haven't Unionist politicians been doing that since Carson brought the union to the brink of civil war and armed his Ulster Volunteer Force with guns and ammunition smuggled in from Germany?

Maeve doesn't really care what Craig does, now that he has

woken Eddie from his torpor. Maeve packs her bags for the hospital.

November

Maeve's mother-in-law is disgusted that the Free State government wants to remove the special position of the Catholic Church, as the guardian of the nation's faith, from the Constitution of Ireland. Maeve doesn't give one continental damn.

Maeve's mother-in-law was born before the partition of Ireland. She remembers a time when the Unionists called themselves Irish. She remembers the War of Independence. She remembers the Black and Tans burning Cork and laying siege to the town of Tralee. She remembers the pogroms in the Belfast shipyards when seven thousand Catholics and 'weak' Protestants were driven from their jobs. Maeve thinks her mother-in-law remembers a damn sight too much.

The Free State government doesn't want to remember. It is looking forward. It is looking to the reunification of the country, which will surely be soon. This situation cannot last; the continuation of the Troubles is unthinkable. The only sensible solution is a united Ireland; half the British government thinks so too. The government in Dublin thinks Northern Ireland's Protestants will feel more welcome in a united future if the Constitution is changed and the special status of the Catholic Church is removed.

Maeve's mother-in-law thinks it's a scandal.

Maeve thinks they should all become Buddhists.

Maeve's husband just wants everyone to give his head peace so he can pick up his daughter and enjoy her.

Maeve has named the baby Catherine. Eddie wonders if she is

named after Kathryn Eakin but he is afraid to ask. Maeve heats the baby's bottle and wishes that her mother-in-law would go home.

December

Maeve opens the bottom door of the corner cabinet and pulls out a bottle of vodka. She takes out the Jameson whiskey, too, and two glasses. Eddie looks up with a start when she stops his gentle snoring with a press of her slippered foot on his.

She has no Coca-Cola to add to her vodka so she has topped up the glass with water. If Eibhlin had come, she would have brought a bottle of Babycham, but Eibhlin has not been invited.

'She has eleven other fucking children. She can go torture someone who doesn't have a six-week-old infant in the house.'

But Maeve had forgotten about the Babycham. She sips at the vodka. It is disgusting, so she takes a longer sip. She reaches across and taps her glass gently against Eddie's.

'Cheers, love.' He takes a sip and grimaces.

'Happy new year,' she whispers as they watch the clock tick towards 1973.

In Dublin, Martin McGuinness has just been arrested under new powers rushed through.

In Derry, the bloodstained carpet is still on the floor of the Top of the Hill bar where five men were murdered ten days ago.

In Omagh, Maeve and Eddie clink their glasses again as the baby stirs in the Moses basket at Eddie's feet.

Eddie has abandoned his scrapbook, but the press have finished their tally. In homes all over Ireland and Britain, a glass is raised to the memory of 479 people, while 4,876 injured lie weeping in their beds at home or in hospital, or sit steely-eyed, sans teeth, sans eyes, sans limbs, sans children, sans everything.

The Sash

Rat–at–tat–tat. Bang. Boom. Boom. Bang.

It is old but it is beautiful …

You look down at the front page of the unsullied newspaper and Paisley's ugly oul' face stares back at you. His jowls are resting on the clerical collar wrapped tight round his neck and he has his bowler hat on. Orangemen are very fond of their bowler hats; they love to give them a good steam and brush-up before the Twelfth and all the other marches they attend each summer.

Christ, you hate your new parish. How in the name of God did you end up here, stuck in the dirty grey streets of a miserable, once-industrial town, hemmed in on all sides by mean little homes full of mean little people? Surely a country parish would have been the obvious choice for a farmer's son?

Before being sent to this god-forsaken dump you had never given a moment's thought to what it felt like to be outnumbered.

Here, in the early months of 1970, while you were safely ensconced in the seminary in Maynooth, the old demographics of the town were swept aside and created anew by the pogroms and the house-burnings. Here, where once the parochial house had been surrounded by mixed streets, Catholic and Protestant going about their quiet lives in wary co-existence, all has changed. The Macs and the Os have fled to the other side of town, leaving the parochial house, St Malachy's Church and the school marooned in an ocean of Orange and of red, white and blue.

Those bloody drums have given you this thumping, pounding headache, and you long to close the blinds and get back into bed. Those bloody drums are out of sync with your heartbeat; they have a lot to answer for.

Of course, as Mattias McAloran, your parish priest, loves to remind you with a frown, the drums are only audible for a few months each year. Surely, Mattias insists, any normal person could accept a wee bit of childish noise for one short third of the year? Mattias suspects that you think you are too good for this kip of a town. Mattias is right.

If only the stress of living were limited to a few months each year. If only the drums *inside* your head were so contained. If you had eight months relief each year from the anxious pounding that ordinary life creates, deep under your own pulse, then you might try to be happy.

Rat-at-tat-tat. Bang. Boom. Boom. Bang.

… and its colours they are fine …

The drums made their first appearance early in spring, your first at St Malachy's. All the children of the neighbourhood spent the lengthening, lazy days playing on the tarmacked road. Their mothers didn't fear a road traffic accident; the men and their cars were at work. The women shopped and carried their groceries in the baskets of giant Silver Cross prams, before their older children turned those massive unwieldy chariots into go-carts and ambulances, stock cars and steam engines.

You had thought, on being given the unwelcome news of your exile to the busy town, that you would at least be able to walk the streets of your new parish and speak with the children, have a laugh, maybe tighten the loose axle of a go-cart, or pass the time of day with the mothers. But that cannot happen here, here where even the youngest children shout and whistle after you, throw stones at your school's pupils, chalk obscenities on the pavement: Fuck the Pope. No Pope Here. Remember 1690.

During the Easter holidays of 1974, you sat on an uncomfortable bench in the back garden of the parochial house enjoying the warmth, respectably covered in black from collar to toes, as dictated by McAloran, and heard for the first time, to your dismay, the rat-at-tat-tat of the bloody drums.

The children had decided it was time for the first parade of the year. Long, long before even the most ardent loyalist climbed into his attic for flags and bunting, the children were out practising their march. Twirling batons made of broom handles entwined with red, white and blue insulation tape, they formed a ragged snake and marched the length of the street. Their lack of prowess with the baton did nothing to dampen their holiday spirits.

You had watched discreetly from the parlour window. Up, up, you followed the arc of the batons into the glare of the low spring sun. They seemed to hang for a moment, then plunge back to earth, three or four at a time. More than once, from your hiding place, you saw the knobbed end of a gaudy stick come hurtling out of the sky, bypassing the outstretched hands of its expectant owner and smash into an upturned face.

At those times you held your breath. Surely this is an end of it? Surely an irate mother will rush out and declare the whole thing to be mad and dangerous? During the weeks that you have already spent hidden behind the parlour curtains, you have heard the women shouting: 'Wait till yer da gets home, he'll skin ya' … 'Don't come running to me when you fall off that bike' … 'Stop that, you wee stumer, you'll put someone's eye out.' Surely these angry women don't consider tossing the caber straight into your own face a suitable pastime for children?

But, it seems, the march is exempt from all normal rules of sense and logic. The owner of the bloodied face is washed and kissed – or occasionally smacked, if he is reckless enough to bleed on a carpet or couch. And so the parade goes on.

Rat-at-tat-tat. Bang. Boom. Boom. Bang.

… It was worn at Derry, Augh-r-rim, Ennis-kill-en and THE
BOYNE …

The shrill soprano voices of the young boys drill into your head, making you think of bamboo shoots that grew through Japanese torture victims in the old black-and-white war movies your father used to like.

Today's march is even noisier than usual, although there is still six weeks to go until the Twelfth. *What the hell is going on out there?* You abandon the *Irish News* on the table, the face of the jowly demagogue glaring out as you once again creep to the curtain. You can't imagine Paisley behaving in this craven fashion; he might not be your idea of a man of God, but he is certainly a man of the people. If Paisley wanted silence, he'd go out and, in the voice of an Old Testament prophet, demand it.

You can see at once why today's parade is so unexpectedly

noisy. Some kindly soul, a DIY enthusiast or a tradesman perhaps, has thoughtfully provided the bandleaders with a load of empty buckets – BAL wall-tile adhesive tubs. They are sturdy, short and squat; their lids don't fly off and splinter; nor do they rebound and lacerate the drummer's wrists, unlike other less robust, less patriotic tubs, emptied of industrial cooking oil and the like. Loops of blue nylon rope and lengths of bamboo stolen from gardens have made Lambeg drums to rival any Grandmaster's.

And it goes on and on.

Rat–at–tat–tat–tat–tat–tat–tat–tat–tat–tat–tat–tat–tat–tat–tat–tat–
tat–tat–tat.

Bang. Boom. Boom. Bang.

... My father wore it as a youth, in bygone days of yore ...

The endless, tuneless, arrhythmic pulse of summer. You don't know whether it's the noise, the lack of skill or the utter selfishness of it all that irks you most. The bright, exalted faces of these marching children are somewhat familiar to you now after months of peering from your window. None are troublemakers in the normal sense of the word. They are the offspring of tough and rigid Presbyterians, well known for their calm, dispassionate use of the belt on their well-behaved sons. Corporal punishment is a matter of pride to them, these descendants of Puritans, even though it is supposedly banned in the schools these days and experts speak out about it. You don't know how they discipline their daughters, who stand at the kerb and cheer their brothers on. Even in childhood games there is no place for women in the Orange Order, not unless they are carrying bottles of Quosh or sandwiches.

Why do you hate the march so much? You know these children don't march past your door to frighten you. They would march whether you were here or not, whether or not you had fled, as is sometimes discussed, to the other end of town where a new Catholic primary school has sprung up to accommodate those whose parents won't risk coming near St Malachy's any more.

You are an irrelevance to the marching children. Their hereditary belief in their inalienable right to walk the 'Queen's highway', their superior demographic entitlement, the success of their fathers' latest strike that brought 'Ulster' to its knees last month, allows them to simply eradicate you from their thoughts. All you have to do is be quiet and allow their world to revolve around them, as it has done since 1690. Nonetheless, even in the absence of malicious intent, you wish to God that they would stop.

Bang. Boom. Boom. Bang.

... And on the Twelfth I love to wear ...

Maybe you will ask Mattias if you can borrow the car on Sunday after all the Masses are over, when the young Catholics are practising Gaelic football at CLG Éire Óg and the young Presbyterians are in Sunday School.

Maybe you could drive the quiet country roads to Drumaleish and visit Alo and his wife, Bid. Bid would give you apple tart and half a yellow cake to bring back in a Quality Street tin. You could walk out into the orchard, or to the meadows to watch the fattening lambs graze. If your mother asks it of you, you could go and stand, blank and dry-eyed, at your father's grave. If your mother asks you, you could tell her how happy you are, how joyful it is to be doing the Lord's work, how good it feels to be in a parish where the people really need a shepherd and the guidance of a strong right hand. And if she smiles and tells her beads for the repose of that miserable oul' bastard Luke O'Donovan, you might start to feel the pulse thrum in your head again.

Rat–at–tat–tat–tat. Bang. Boom. Boom. Bang.

… The-e farm my bro-oth-er owns …

Wake up, Mammy

:::::

Mary-Ann Gillen lifted a rake of hand towels out of her sister's hot press, choosing the oldest and tattiest, the ones with the binding coming away from the edges or grey in the centre from years of wiping the half-washed oil- or dung-encrusted hands of Bid's husband, Alo.

Mary-Ann's husband, a veteran of twenty years in the boning-hall at Mackle's abattoir, had warned her to do something about the kitchen floor. 'It's like the side of a fuckin' bottle it's that slippery,' Dan had said. 'It's alright for me used to doing the slaughterhouse shuffle, but someone else is going to go arse over tit if we're not careful.' He was right – the last thing Alo O'Donovan needed was a visitor breaking their ankle in his house, today of all days.

Dan grabbed the handful of towels from his wife, threw two down onto the faded, scored lino of Bid's floor and stepped carefully into the centre of each one. He glided around the kitchen floor on them, out into the scullery and back entry, then returned, trailing a streak of dampness behind him.

'Find one of the young lads to do that, Dan, and go you on into the bedroom.'

Mary-Ann knew she was a lucky woman to have a husband who even noticed a slippery, wet kitchen floor, let alone actually do something about it, but still and all, a woman doesn't like to see her man doing housework, not in front of his friends. Next thing he'd be drying the dishes.

Dan grabbed one of their four sons and handed over the clean towels. 'Take that puss off yer face and help yer mother,' he said. 'It's not every day a woman wakes her only sister.'

Mary-Ann turned round to face the stove, blinking furiously, and when she turned back, Dan was gone up to the bedroom to make sure no one caught sight of Bid's body left unattended. Her son stood on two dry towels, waiting. The late unexpected April snow, carried in as filthy grey clumps on the feet of the mourners, melted on the floor and mingled with the condensation that dripped from the low, plastered ceiling. Clouds of steam belched from four giant kettles hopping on the hotplates of the stove. The whole room was like laundry day in hell. If they didn't keep the floor dry, there would be an accident for sure. Opening the window wasn't an option – it would freeze the horns off a moily cow out there.

'Right, Mammy,' said her eldest boy from the scullery door where he was acting as look-out, 'here comes the team now.'

Cars crunched over the gravel; doors slammed open and shut. The hubbub of men's voices approached. Mary-Ann hoisted up one of the kettles and poured boiling water into three already scalded teapots.

'Grab them sandwiches,' she ordered. 'And you, Tommy, get ready with them towels – the place'll be like a skating rink after this crowd passes through.'

Seamus Kelly, the club Chairman, came first, hands outstretched, clutching a Mass card and a box of USA biscuits.

'I'm sorry for yer trouble, Mary-Ann.' He handed her the biscuits while awkwardly shaking her other hand and looking around for Alo. 'Come on in with them chairs,' he called and the senior team of Drumaleish GAA club trooped in, each man carrying a folding chair from the clubhouse.

'Sorry for yer loss.'

'Sorry for yer trouble.'

'Sorry ...'

'Sorry ...'

Sorry ... sorry ... sorry. Mary-Ann lost track of names and faces, variously smiling nervously or composed into careful expressions of sympathy. Most of the senior team were too young to have buried anyone more valued than an aged grandparent or great-uncle. What would they know about the loss of a sister?

'And is Alo around?' asked Seamus.

'He's out in the fields with the little one, keeping him out from under everyone's feet. You know how it is. This damn snow, out of the blue. Some of the neighbours are helping him to bring the youngstock into the barn. Be just as easy as trying to feed them in the fields.'

'Of course, of course.' Seamus nodded, and then Molly Murphy bustled in from the hall, full of orders, and the team followed in her fussy wake, dropping off an extra chair or two in each of the rooms as she instructed. Seamus followed them, and Mary-Ann heard Dan greet him and draw him upstairs to the bedroom where Bid was in repose. Thank God for Dan, she thought. Where the hell was Alo, and what was he playing at, messing around on the land and his wife, her sister, dead in the bed upstairs? Mary-Ann needed Alo here, shaking hands, nodding, doing the right thing.

Two more soaking filthy towels were dropped into the basket beside her and two dry ones were readied for the next influx of visitors.

'Who in the name of Jesus is that ringing at the front door?' muttered Mary-Ann. 'Who the hell thinks we've nothing better to do, today of all days, than open the front door to them?'

'It's Father O'Donovan,' called her youngest boy from the other end of the house. 'Mammy, Father O'Donovan is here.'

'Mother of God, give me strength. Talk about pick yer moment,' she muttered. 'Right, well that's okay, love,' she shouted back as she smoothed her hair. 'I'll be up in a minute. Bring Father upstairs.' She looked around the emptying kitchen. 'Tommy, leave them towels for a minute. Get out there and find yer Uncle Alo and tell him I'll skin him if he doesn't come straight back with you. Father O'Donovan is here for the rosary.'

She found Anthony O'Donovan upstairs in the small front room that had been his parents' bedroom and that now belonged to Alo and Bid. The old-fashioned mahogany dressing table and bedside lockers were almost black with age and furniture polish, and the matching bedstead loomed large in the room.

Anthony was rummaging in a small black briefcase.

'Do you mind?' he asked. 'I brought a few of my own bits and pieces? Do you mind?'

In his hand he held a beautiful brass crucifix and on the table sat a matching pair of candlesticks and a crystal holy water dispenser. Beside them, Bid's crucifix looked cheap and tawdry, stainless steel with a plain glass font below.

'I don't mind, Father – '

'Anthony, please.'

She gave him a little nod. 'But I don't know what Alo will say.'

'They were a gift from our mother on my ordination day.'

'They're lovely, so they are, but Alo might prefer to use Bid's.'

But, when Alo finally dragged himself and Cormac back into the wake room, he didn't even notice.

Hail Mary, full of grace …

Every inch of floor was occupied. One thing about dying young, thought Mary-Ann, there are plenty left alive to mourn you. There'd be a bloody scrum tomorrow to shoulder the coffin. There would have to be at least ten lifts, with six men to a lift, to give everyone who wanted to be seen a chance to shoulder. Or maybe four men to a lift and let them carry her the whole way – it was only half a mile. But could Mary-Ann take the stress of watching the lifts change, every man slipping his shoulder out from underneath, creating another chance to drop the coffin?

As for getting her sister downstairs tomorrow, there was no way on earth Mary-Ann could stomach watching that. She had seen Bid's mother-in-law taken down them stairs two years earlier, the coffin hoisted over the banisters from the tiny landing, no room for niceties, and then carried almost vertical down the steep flight of steps, the men straining and quietly cursing. It certainly wasn't the first time Mary-Ann had ever heard the F-word, but she didn't want to hear it tomorrow as Bid left her home for the last time.

The Lord is with thee …

The bedroom door was open. Mourners packed the landing outside and spilled down the stairs into the hallway. Mary-Ann's four boys were down there, despite her strict instructions to make sure they got a space in the room with their dead aunt. If she heard later that they had been acting the lig instead of respectfully answering the rosary, she'd give them all a thick ear.

Blessed art thou amongst women …

Bid looked shocking. There was no other word for it, really;

no point trying to butter that parsnip. She looked what she was, a skeleton, with the driest, paper-thin layer of skin stretched across bones from which every ounce of muscle had melted away in the space of four months. Mary-Ann had heard the other women lying to each other – *Oh she looks beautiful. Ach she's at peace now. She doesn't look a day older than her wedding day* – and wondered who the hell they were trying to fool. It's not as easy as all that to die in your thirties, thought Mary-Ann. It takes some starving to stop a thirty-five-year-old heart, even if you do have ovarian cancer.

The bed looked great though. Molly Murphy had helped with it, carefully folding and tucking the three folds of the undersheet, representing the three steps to heaven, the holy trinity, the three leaves of St Patrick's shamrock. It looked like it had been tucked by a machine. Molly never missed a wake. It was practically her hobby.

And blessed is the fruit of thy womb …

Bid had been betrayed by her womb. Six years childless, then three years after Cormac was born and still not a sign of another pregnancy. Mary-Ann had looked at her four fine sons growing like docks in a ditch and shook her head. What were Alo and Bid playing at? Sure Cormac would be half-reared before the brother or sister came along. Meanwhile, Bid's left ovary had been eating her up in the dark, silent recesses of her belly.

Holy Mary, mother of God …

Bid had picked out the bed linen before she died, the same Belfast linen in which their own parents, Mick and Ita Hendron, had been laid out. She had been very firm about it. 'I don't want the O'Donovan funeral linens. I was ashamed of my life of them at Alo's mother's wake. That woman hadn't a clue how to launder linen nor how to store it. It's as yella as a duck's foot. You wouldn't even give it to St Vincent de Paul.'

Mary-Ann had brought over the hundred-year-old Hendron

linen and they had chosen it together – pillow cases, sheets and incidentals – which Mary-Ann boiled and dried out of direct sunlight, ironing it while still damp, until her sister was satisfied that her last bed would be white enough.

Pray for us sinners …

Precious little chance Bid had ever got to sin, Mary-Ann thought. She looked at her brother-in-law, who was as white as the bed his wife lay upon, and at the child wriggling and struggling in his arms. Forty-two years old, married for ten, a father for three, a widower now.

He had never given Bid any reason for complaint, not as far as Mary-Ann knew, and she would have known. Alo had put in a telephone after the wedding in 1967 so that Bid could talk to her sister. Not every man would have done that, especially a man who was as careful with money as Alo.

Oh, my Jesus, have mercy on us. Save us from the fires of hell …

How could Anthony O'Donovan stand there, younger than his dead sister-in-law, and talk to them about the fires of hell? How could he even bring himself to mention the fires of hell in this room, in relation to this dead saint, this woman who had never had a thought for herself, who led a blameless life and had been rewarded with an excruciating and torturous end? Mary-Ann felt the first twinges of doubt. Where was the consolation she had been promised? Why was the kindest and best sister who ever walked God's earth lying in a shroud aged thirty-five when Dan's mother, that oul' bitch with a face on her like a slapped arse and a heart cold as charity, was still going strong in her eighty-fifth year?

In the name of the Father, and of the Son, and of the Holy Spirit. Amen.

Across the sea of people, across the moment of contemplative silence while the mourners wondered who would be the first to leave the room, to ask for tea, to choose a scone thickly slathered with jam, Bid's child's voice rang out.

'Time to get up now, Mammy. Wake up. Wake up, Mammy. Daddy, tell Mammy she's been in bed long enough.'

Mary-Ann pushed her way out through the crowded doorway and into the bathroom where the only uncovered mirror in the house showed her a glimpse of her face, just as it collapsed.

Sparky

::::::

I finally find the car keys on the bottom shelf of the fridge underneath the chipped blue and white jug of milk I'd carried in from the parlour this morning. I had been tearing the house apart trying to find them, silently effing and blinding. Only the look of horror on the face of President Kennedy stopped me from blurting it all out. He's hanging there, near the Sacred Heart and the Papal Seal on the certificate of blessing that Bid's mother got for us before we tied the knot.

The cream on the milk is already rising and coalescing round the long blade of grass that I dropped in out of force of habit. Fuck knows what I think I'm going to do with it. It's not like anyone's going to carefully skim the precious top-of-the-milk off into a clean jug and pour it over freshly baked apple tart for me. Those days are gone. The neighbours have moved on to the next tragedy – never short of one around here – and I'm feeding myself and the child these days, God help the poor wee bastard. I sure as hell won't be trying to bake a tart, although a world of last autumn's apples lies out there, eaters and cookers, rotting on the orchard floor. After Bid got her news, neither of us could muster the energy to harvest them.

So there'll be no tarts.

In any case, thon fucking stove is driving me to distraction. It's a bloody tyrant! Every time I open the door it's to find the fire either a grey demoralising pile of ash or a roaring furnace from which Beelzebub himself would recoil. I doubt an apple tart will ever be cooked in thon machine again.

Why don't you get a wee girl to come in and help? I've been asked that same question more times than I can remember. Women's faces, peering up at me, maybe with a daughter or a niece already in mind for the cushy number as a widower's housekeeper. To be honest, I can't even think of a reasonable answer to give them. *Sure, it's the obvious thing to do, and it'd be putting a few quid into the hand of a girl who needs it. Didn't Bid have the insurance policy?* I have to bite my lip and turn away for fear I'll put my hand through the door or punch the puss of the next woman who asks me that.

It's not just the money – I wouldn't object to giving a lassie a few quid – it's the implication. *He's not able to manage thon child.* That's what they really mean and what they say to each other when they see Cormac at Mass on a Sunday, his wee trousers just that bit too short on him, or his face, that I wiped thirty seconds before getting into the car, crusted in snot and God knows what else. *Daughter dear, I'm asking you, how could a man, let alone a dairy farmer, look after a wean on his own? Don't we know the men are useless under it all? Poor Bid must be turning in her grave.*

I stare at the keys in the fridge and try to remember what in hell I wanted them for in the first place. Was I heading out to the shop? It must be nigh on dinner time. I'm well able to steam a pot of spuds and a few carrots on the hotplate, but ovens are beyond me. How in the name of God did Bid manage it? It's a curse of a yoke. Little wonder she'd spent her years gently begging for an

Electrolux cooker from McGreal's in the town. Every time we passed the shop, she'd stared in the window – blue and white, with an eye-level grill; it didn't look like any cooker I'd ever seen. I didn't fancy the idea of grilled food. Sure didn't the big frying pan on the hotplate cook a steak to perfection, and even if the dinner was only a few rashers, how would she fry the soda bread if all the grease was grilled away?

'Do you see it has the one big oven, a small one, and a warming drawer at the bottom?' she'd said.

'Do you think I'm made of money? Do you think I'd be breaking my back chopping logs and kindling if we had the money for a brand new electric stove?'

'You wouldn't have to break yer back if I just had to flick a switch.'

'Aye, and then the electricity bill would break it for me.'

Naturally, a man would like to get his woman the cooker she was hankering for. Naturally, I would. But three years ago I'd been hankering for a new reversible plough. And when the plough was bought, I'd needed a new pump for the washer in the dairy. And after the washer it was roll bars and a cab for the old Massey so I was following the new safety guidelines of the Ulster Farmers Union. Bid had nodded when I told her about the tractor cab.

'That's the right job, Alo. I'll be happy to see you inside the cab in the dry, and safe under the roll bars.' She always fretted about me. 'Farming's full of dangers, love. You get the tractor up til the Union guidelines. Where would we be if you broke yer leg – or worse?'

'That's right, pet, and when that job's done we'll talk about the cooker.'

I reach into the fridge for the keys and drop them into the pocket of my overalls where they should have been all along. I'll go into town and buy a couple of loaves. God, the shop-bought bread is desperate, like wallpaper paste turned solid and sliced, but it'll have to do. I've spent so long staring into the fridge, there'll be no time for boiling spuds the day.

I go into the living room where Cormac is safely watching Lenny the Lion. Thank God Lenny is teaching the reading now. I don't think I could take it if we still had to tune in to *Listen with Mother*. Luckily I've persuaded Cormac that it's too old-fashioned. Sure, if I sat down in her chair with Cormac on my lap to listen, I might never be able to get up again. If it wasn't for Cormac and the thought of the poor cows' milk dripping down their legs in the mornings, I'd never get out of bed again.

'C'mon,' I say, scooping him up. 'We're heading into town.'

I don't realise I'm crying until Cormac points at my face and I taste the snot on my tongue.

::::::

The two pan loaves hang limp like dead rabbits from my hand. I throw some jam and marmalade into a basket and set the pale skittery oul' bread on top of them.

'Can I have some sweets, Daddy?'

'Away outta that. On a Tuesday? No chance.'

'Ah please. Please please please pretty please with sugar and jam on.'

'Here you are, Cormac love.' Monica McCaffrey's bosom nearly bursts through her tight nylon shop coat as she leans across the high counter and puts a couple of Refreshers into Cormac's outstretched mitt. 'Just a wee lock of chews for the wee pet, Alo,' she says.

To be honest, I'm grateful to her for saving me the row and the inevitable loss of face when I give in to the child. Half the women in town are in cahoots about how Cormac and I should live our lives, but Monica's heart is in the right place, no matter how well padded her chest might be. She wouldn't bang her nose if she tripped over, that's for sure. *Ha! I must tell Bid that when I get home. That'll give her a good laugh.*

Fuck! What is wrong with me?

Cormac has the papers ripped off all his sweets, and has one in his mouth and the other two resting sticky in his hand. His little jaws are barely up to the job of chewing a whole Refresher. He can't even answer me – just gives me a thumbs up when I tell him it's time to go. My head is still reeling from the shock of once again realising that Bid is dead. How much time must elapse before I stop turning to her chair or looking up to catch her eye?

It's been four months already. The snowdrops had long since lost their petals and the tulips had just started to open. I had brought a handful of daffodils into the bedroom every day to freshen the vase beside her. There wasn't much else above the ground. I don't think I'll ever again be able to thole an indoor daffodil.

We kept her in our own double bed right up to a few days before the end so I could climb in beside her and hold her close on the days when she wasn't tired to her bones. Many's the day she was so sore I just let the tips of my fingers touch the tips of hers, until she pulled them away with a tiny gurn. Cormac rolled around on the lino beside the bed, banging his Matchbox cars into the skirting boards until I thought the noise was going to drive me to drink. It poisoned me to think of the fitted carpet Bid had had in her bedroom at her mother's house.

'What would you be putting carpet in a farmhouse for, love?' I'd argued. 'Waste of money and it'd be filthy in no time.'

'But you never come further into the house than the scullery without taking off yer boots, Alo,' she'd said. 'And I'd like the feel of warm carpet on my feet in the early hours when the baby needs feeding.'

'I still say it'd be a dirt trap, Bid love. Maybe we'll talk about it after I've paid off the new hay-bob.'

Of course, despite my momentary lapses when I look for her, or open my mouth to tell her a funny story, I know I'm not crazy. I know she's dead. Sure aren't we at the graveside every Sunday after Mass, and doesn't Cormac remind me often enough.

Mammy's dead, Daddy.

Mammy's dead. Mrs Keenan said she was a beautiful corpse. Not a bit too dolled-up. Very like herself. Isn't that nice, Daddy?

Mammy's in a big hole in the ground until Jesus brings us all up to Heaven. Will Fluffy be in Heaven too, Daddy?

Mammy's dead and all happy now, looking after us from heaven.

'Would you houl' yer whist, for the love of Jesus!' I say, but thinking *shut the fuck up!* So far I've managed not to say the last bit out loud.

::::::

Cormac is wriggling and twisting and I look down to realise that I'm squeezing the blood out of his little hand; his chin is wobbling too. I hunker down beside him on the street and peel the last remaining Refresher out of his other hand and make as if to stuff it into my own gob. The howl of rage distracts him from his sore fingers, and then he starts to laugh when he's absolutely sure I'm only messing with him.

'Come on, Cormac, we've one more job to do.'

Swinging the bag with the jam and bread in my right hand and carefully taking his tiny paw in my left, we set off up the high street.

'Where are we going now? I'm hungry and I want my sandwich.'

'It won't take long.'

McGreal's isn't the best electrical shop in town and I'd be surprised if it's the cheapest, but the other one is owned by a member of the Royal Black Preceptory, and Drew McIvor can kiss my Fenian hole if he thinks he's getting one penny out of me. There's at least two of everything in town, one Orange, one Green, even if there's scarce the trade to keep one open. It's like a shopping version of apartheid, only it's self-inflicted and self-policed.

Anyway, I went to school with Peadar McGreal, or *Peter* as he was called then, back when the Council jobs all went to Orangemen and the births and deaths registrars wouldn't deal with names in the Irish language. I'd look well giving my money to someone who would tell a father how to name his own child instead of giving it to Peadar.

'I'll do you the very best price I can, Alo,' Peadar's young lad Patsy says after the first clumsy greetings and condolences. *Still?* he's probably thinking to himself. *Is thon oul' eejit still moping about the place? Sure it's months since the wife died. Jesus, he'd want to get a grip on himself.*

And I know he's not alone in thinking that. Life goes on apparently.

Grief should come with an off switch. I wish to fuck it did. Then I wouldn't be standing here with two fat tears sizzling on the hotplate of this cursèd blue and white Electrolux cooker, and Patsy McGreal wouldn't have to pretend he hasn't noticed. I reach over and flick the switch and try to act like a man.

'That'll do fine, Patsy. And you've one in stock? Bring it out to me tomorrow or the day after.'

'You'll need a sparky, Alo,' he says, calling me by my name, the young pup, and him barely twenty year old. 'You can't just plug a powerful yoke like this into the socket. It'll blow the house to kingdom come and fuck your wiring.'

'Okay. I'll leave that to your da to organise. Get it sorted and let me know.'

The days are long gone when I had too much pride to let another man labour in my house. If the Electrolux needs a sparky, Peadar can organise it. I'll sit in Bid's chair in the kitchen like an oul' doll and watch as the sparky wires the cooker in, and I'll let the real men tell me how to live.

It would help if I could just stop fucking crying.

Christmas in October

::::::

'Cathy McGrain, where is your lunchbox?'

Cathy looked down at her empty hands and then up, innocence radiating from her big blue eyes. Attracta McAliskey, the lunch room and playground supervisor, waited for an answer.

'I've forgotten my lunch, Mrs McAliskey,' whispered Cathy. 'I'll just sit here and do without. Mebbe one of the girls would give me a drink of water.' *Please let me go to the canteen. Please let me go to the canteen.*

Cathy's lunch was carefully hidden at the bottom of her bed, tucked under the bedspread. She wanted to try a delicious hot dinner from the school canteen. *It's not bloody fair. Even Sarah Brady gets to eat school dinner. Why does my family never get anything?*

And it was true, they never got *anything*. Cathy's father, Eddie, earned just enough to disqualify his children from free school uniforms and free school meals. They didn't get a bus pass, so they had to walk to school come rain or snow. They didn't get a free Halloween party, paid for by the social, and St Vincent de Paul never brought them coal at Christmas, although they were cold enough to want it.

'It would sicken yer happiness,' Cathy's mother would say. 'It's enough to make a body quit work altogether and go on the brew. To see other people's children getting everything, and the parents lying on their holes watching TV and smoking all day long.'

Cathy's father would snort in disgusted agreement. 'Wouldn't it just poison you?' Then he would polish his work shoes to an even higher shine.

Please let me go to the canteen. Just this once.

'This won't do Cathy, you can't sit all day on an empty stomach. Why didn't you tell Sister Oliver and we could have phoned your mother?'

Cathy's mother would have searched the kitchen and hallway for the missing lunchbox to no avail. Then how could Cathy reintroduce the lunchbox to the kitchen cupboard? It had taken months of pleading to get the lunchbox in the first place, months of trying to explain that Cathy was *the only girl in the whole school* who carried her lunch to school in the plastic wrapper of the Ormo sliced pan loaf. It was bad enough having to eat the bloody sandwiches without everyone knowing she couldn't afford a proper lunchbox.

'Maybe I could go to the canteen?' Cathy said. She was pretty sure Mrs McAliskey wouldn't make her sit empty-handed in the lunchroom, and sure what else could be done at this short notice?

Please let me go to the canteen.

Maybe it was true what Noeleen and Sonia said, that the school dinners their parents paid for were actually worse than nothing and that the stew was bulked out with the boke of sick children in the local hospital.

Let me just try it for once and then I'll know. Surely to God, it couldn't be worse than ham sandwiches?

God, how Cathy hated ham! The thin, almost transparent slices, glistening with unspeakable jelly. Boke. Worse was the slimy rim of lurid yellow crumb. Worser still was the crunch of white gristle between her teeth. Boke. Boke. Boke.

Lorna, the kind lady behind the counter at McEvoy's butcher, often set aside the tail end of a breaded ham for Cathy's mother. The little nubs were too small and fiddly to bother pushing through the slicing machine. Big fat Lorna would drop the nubs into the bag along with the slices – fifteen slices every week – and wink at Maeve. Her drooping jowls would quiver as she smiled conspiratorially. On those days, Cathy wanted to die.

'It's the least she could do,' Cathy's mother would snap, 'the amount of money I spend in there every week.'

Fifteen slices of ham every week. Three rounds of Ormo ham sandwiches every day, Monday to Friday: Cathy, Liam and Mark. When things were good, the bread would have butter. When things were tight, it was Flora margarine.

Couldn't Cathy maybe, just some days, have cheese? Just for a wee change? No, ham was better for growing children. And what was wrong with the ham? Freshly sliced ham from a butcher, not out of a packet? Did Cathy think ham grew on trees? Did Cathy think her father was working himself to the bone so Cathy could turn her nose up at butcher's ham when children in Africa were starving to death? If Cathy thought she was too good for ham, maybe she would prefer caviar?

As a reminder that things could always – always – get worse, there were days when her mother reached for the Plumrose Chopped Ham: tinned, spiced, sliding glutinously out of its container with a sickening slurp. On the weeks when the fifteen slices could not be stretched until Friday, perhaps when an unexpected visitor called to the house, prompting frantic sandwich-making and the sending of a child helter-skelter to McKeevney's shop for a packet of Bourbon Creams, Cathy's mother would reach into the larder and produce an emergency tin of Plumrose Chopped Ham. On those days Cathy's lunch could not even be salvaged by the usual means of removing the hated ham and eating the bread. Plumrose Chopped Ham sullied everything it touched, its ghastly juices soaking deep into every nook and cranny of the innocent bread.

'Will I go to the canteen, so?' asked Cathy.

Mrs McAliskey took a quare gunk at her and rolled her eyes behind her big owl-glasses. 'Certainly not. You can't eat a school lunch you haven't paid for. That won't work. The potatoes are bought and peeled depending on how many lunches are paid for on a Monday.' Suddenly her face brightened. 'You'll have to go over to the convent. Run along to the kitchen door – it's the one beside Sister Martin's room – and tell them you've no lunch.'

What? You cannot be fucking serious? Eat my lunch in the nun's kitchen?

'It's alright, Mrs McAliskey, I'm not even really that hungry.'

'Nonsense.' The woman was all smiles now – problem solved, disaster averted. 'Run over to the kitchen quick. The lunch is half over and you still empty.'

'I'll be fine –'

'Go now, for heaven's sake, and stop dawdling. Run!'

Cathy slammed out of the lunchroom and ran across the yard. She paused with her hand on the wrought-iron gate that separated the playground from the convent garden. To her left lay the nuns' graveyard. She could just duck in there for twenty minutes. She took a quick juke around but no one was watching her. Would anyone be any the wiser? Would oul' bootface McAliskey think of double-checking? In the end she was too cowed, too institutionalised to disobey.

She pushed the gate open and trailed her feet to the pair of doors in the basement of the convent. One led to Sister Martin's room, where the slow girls revised *The cat sat on the mat* and the six times tables; the other, never broached before, led to the kitchen.

'What is it, child?' asked the elderly nun who answered her knock.

She's easily a hundred years old, thought Cathy. She didn't know the nun's name or recognise her face. She didn't teach in the school, or come across to demonstrate knitting or needlework. She didn't even appear for the May procession when the statue of Our Lady was carried around the nuns' graveyard and the girls walked behind carrying flowers and singing hymns. Maybe this nun was a prisoner in the basement, nameless, never seeing the sun or feeling the wind on her face.

'Come in, come in, you wee pet.' A big smile creased the old nun's deeply wrinkled cheeks. 'You must be starving. Sit yourself down beside the range.'

Heat belted out from the big cast-iron cooker, which had several pots rattling and hopping on the hotplates. A glass of creamy cold milk appeared as if by magic in the nun's hand, and Cathy took it from her and sipped gratefully.

'Forgotten your lunch, daughter dear, and you working away over in school with your stomach thinking your throat's been cut.' The nun was opening and closing cupboards, pulling a long, vicious-looking knife out of a drawer. 'I'll sort you out in two shakes of a lamb's tail.' She smiled and opened the door of a huge floor-to-ceiling pantry. 'How about a nice ham sandwich?'

Fuck. Fuck. Think, for fuck's sake.

'I'm actually a vegetarian, Sister.'

'A what, dear?'

'A vegetarian, Sister. It means I don't eat meat.'

'Don't eat meat? I've never heard such oul' guff. Your mother should be ashamed, allowing such nonsense.'

Cathy thought of the fifteen slices of ham and the fact that her mother never ate one, never ate – nor got the chance to eat – the five slices of ham that every week her ungrateful daughter crammed down the side of the lunchroom bin, or gave away to another girl. She thought about her mother hacking at the little nubs of leftover ham from Lorna, salvaging whatever could be trimmed off for her own lunch. A tear sprang up in the corner of Cathy's eye.

'Ach, don't! Don't be crying,' said the old nun. 'My bark's worse than my bite. Do you know what that means?' Cathy nodded. 'Good girl. Just wait a wee minute and you'll be as right as rain.'

Jesus, two clichés in the one breath. Sister Oliver would take away marks for that. Cathy nodded again and tried to smile.

The nun bustled about, sawing two thick cuts off a crusty loaf and covering them with as much butter as Cathy's mother would have divided between the six daily slices of Ormo. *That's perfect. That's enough. Don't destroy it with ham!*

Next, a huge platter was banged down onto the table. Cathy stared at it in wonder. On the platter a large pink ham sat resplendent, its rind blackened and sticky with a honey glaze. It was a Christmas ham, a 'Turkey and Ham' ham, even though it was only October.

The nun hacked an enormous slice off the joint and placed it between the lavishly buttered slices of bread.

'Drink up your milk and eat your sandwich, daughter dear, and hurry back to your classroom. The sisters'll be finishing their own lunch now at one o'clock and I need to clear the dining room.'

Cathy bit into the bread. It was a taste explosion! The salty butter and the honey-sweetened ham. The cold fresh milk. The dense, nutty, nearly black crust of the bread. For the first time

Cathy realised that a slice of ham could mean a slice *off* a ham, a Christmas ham.

At three o'clock Cathy didn't have time to think about the unfairness of life as the other girls with their bus passes or their fifteen-pence bus fare were left behind by her flying feet. She was round the corner and out of sight within seconds. She burst through the door of the house and flew into the kitchen.

'Mammy, wait'll you hear. My lunch got wet from my water bottle and I had to eat lunch in the convent kitchen. The nun gave me a ham sandwich, cut off a Christmas ham – the nuns eat Christmas ham all the year round.'

Her mother turned from the sink, turnip in one hand, knife in the other. 'I'm uneasy about them,' she snapped. 'I'd like to see them feed five people on thirty pounds a week.'

The Visit

:::::

In the seconds before the visitor pulls a balaclava over his five o'clock shadow you already know he is bad news. A solitary figure slouching up the long farm path, no friendly wave, no shouted greeting. Skin-tight denim – *drainpipes*, your father would have called them. No dungarees, no boiler suit. You know this is not the unrecognised younger son of a neighbour come to borrow a half pound of staples for a barbed-wire fence.

Just before his face swims into focus, he pauses and pulls on the mask, taking all your attention, and you gasp in amazement as two other wraiths materialise from the shadows behind you.

Strangers on your land, in your yard. How strange are they? Let's find out.

'*Dia daoibh*,' you say, strong and loud.

'May God and Mary be with you,' replies the first stranger.

The words in the Irish language roll off his lips without thought, as automatic as the responses at Mass on Sunday. If you had intoned 'The Lord be with you', he would have chanted back 'And also with you'. The man behind you to your left is more fluent still; 'God's blessing upon the work' is his reply. The third man is silent.

Before, you knew nothing about your visitors. Now you know something. Catholic, Republican, Catholic-educated, Belfast accents. They might be graduates of the University of Long Kesh, where all the Republican prisoners only speak Irish, thwarting their Unionist prison guards, clinging desperately to this hint of dignity. IRA, INLA, IPLO – some outfit like that. The bulges in the men's coats are more obvious now; they have shifted their stance to bring the outline of the weapons into sharp relief against their cheap nylon bomber jackets, but they have not produced them. Yet.

You are alone on the farm. Where is Baby? He is locked in the shed and you are glad he is safe. You have played many a good game with Baby, but you do not want to play it now.

When the Jehovah's Witnesses call to the farm, you always give them five minutes to talk. Five minutes is not too long to ask of any man. When the time has elapsed, you gently suggest that you will return to your labours, that they will go home. Two minutes later, if their stiff, black overcoats have not folded back into the red Datsun Cherry, you interrupt them. *Sorry, lads, I need to feed my little dog.* At the first sound of his name, Baby comes charging into the front yard. Saliva drools from his powerful chops and splatters on the ground. Jehovah's friends gasp or cry out as the Dobermann slips and slides to a halt, claws grating beside your Wellington boot. The pamphlets drop to the ground as the men struggle back into the small car, and you pick the papers up and hand them back, smiling. *Sorry, lads, Baby hates waiting for his meal.*

Yes, you are glad the dog is locked up. These trigger-happy city boys will shoot him at first sight, before the first rich, bowel-loosening bay escapes his throat, and they will almost certainly make a mess of the shot; no clean death that a noble animal such as Baby deserves.

You are alone.

The men are slow to speak, they are out of their milieu. You have noted the involuntary wince, the twitch of disgust as Number One planted his shiny, black shoe into a barely crusted cowpat on the laneway. Such impractical footwear – *winkle-pickers*, your dad would have called them.

They do not intend to kill you – you would be dead by now. Why would they kill you, one of their own, minding your business, bothering no one? What do they want?

At length, Number Three speaks, the sing-song, nasal accent you have heard on the nightly news for two decades now, detailing the litany of woe; hard vowels, missing consonants, no country softness in this voice.

'Now, Mr O'Donovan, we're here for a tractor and a dung-spreader. No need for any unpleasantness. A wee donation to the war effort is all.'

'The war effort, lads? But I'm not at war. A wee mistake maybe? Maybe we'll all go back to our business and forget this *wee* misunderstanding?'

Number Three replies from the closeness of your right elbow. He does not touch you, but he is close, so close. 'Not at war, Mr, O'Donovan? The country is at war. The machinery will be put to good use against the enemies of the Irish Republican Army.'

'Enemies, you say? Yes, enemies. Farmers have many enemies, boys. Drought is my enemy and more so the endless rain and inundation. Lack of fodder following a wet summer is my battle, and the winter frost that turns the poached fields to rutted iron is my nemesis. I have no human foe, unless you mean the men in the co-op who set the price for the milk so low that I can bare squeeze a living from the good land my father left me. I think you've come to the wrong place.'

Numbers One and Two gawp and titter at you. Their mouths are open – *catching flies*, your father called it. They glance uneasily to their leader for guidance. Slowly and with menace, he claps his hands together, a bitter ovation. A thick gob of tobacco-brown phlegm lands on the concrete half an inch from your boot, preceding his words, calm, measured.

'All well and good there, Hamlet. Ten outta ten for the composition. Nice use of vocabulary there. Yer teachers must be proud of you. They might be prouder still if you did your duty there and gave us the weapons we need to progress the war. Nathin' has been said yet that can't be unsaid.'

In the small haggard beside the house a full line of washing flutters in the wind. The empty trouser legs and the flapping shirts bring into sharp recall a woodcut you saw long ago in an old book: a gibbet, its swinging, decaying scraps of bird-pecked humanity and wind-torn clothing blurred indistinctly into one. Will you end up as a propaganda woodcut for a new generation, a photo in tomorrow's *Irish News*, a misshapen heap on a wheeled gurney on the bedtime news?

Under the laden clothes line a swoop of swallows, a hundred strong, frantically peck, seeking worms, seeds, roots – anything that will sustain them on their journey back to Africa, away out of this mad hellhole. You know that any moment now this massed gathering of rats on wings will take fright and take flight and, with a sound like the rattle of distant machine-gun fire, will wheel up and away over your heads. You know that the visitors will jump and flinch – *taking their eye off the ball*, your father called it. If you are to take a chance, a fight or flight, it must be then.

'What time is it, boys?'

Whatever is to happen, it must happen before Cormac comes cycling back from the Sacred Heart College in Omagh. You know that if the boy comes home, you are lost. You know that if the men speak to your motherless son, if they casually touch one inch of his precious skin, or ruffle his hair in jest, you are lost.

You see it unfold in your mind's eye in slow motion, a premonition of the certainty of things to come. The man reaches out to touch your child, to take his bicycle from him, to inspire him in this heroic adventure against the enemies of God, motherland and nature. You see yourself pivot and turn. Your teak-hard fist falls, like the sledgehammer you wielded all day yesterday, against the skull of this frail city weakling. Number Two you take down with a kick to the back of the knee, stamping and grinding your heel into his face, crushing his Belfast whine with your toe on his windpipe. Number One is lifted from the ground by the impact of your shoulder, massive from five decades of bullock-wrestling. Or else he has managed to extract his gun by now and has ended you. Either way, dead or in prison, murdered or murderer, you leave the boy behind, alone. Orphaned.

Whatever is to happen must happen soon.

'Mr O'Donovan, we don't have all day. There's an easy way and a hard way. We need the keys. Giz the keys, Mr O'Donovan, and then have a wee sit-down in a chair with a hankie in yer mouth for a few hours. It's not much to ask.'

You know these men have never set foot on a farm before. It is no easy matter for a novice to hitch a muck-spreader to a tractor, working by instinct, one toe on the accelerator, the length of the body at full stretch, twisted and hoisted, head out the rear window. If you are clever, and brave, this could work out.

'The keys are in my pocket, boys. I won't give them to you. I daresay you'll be able to take them eventually.'

No one has drawn a gun yet, but the faceless men are sighing and flexing their fingers. Whatever happens, you must not get shot. You must not go to hospital with a *six-pack*, bullets lodged in your knees, elbows and ankles. You must get away with a clean deception.

'Alo! Quit acting the fuckin' maggot. Giz the keys and you won't get hurt. Three armed men against one? No need to act the fuckin' hero. No blame on an innocent farmer tied up and threatened by three masked men with guns.'

No more *Mr O'Donovan*, then. Is that good or bad, you wonder.

'Lads, I feel sure it won't be necessary to get the armoury out. What would people say? Shooting one of your own? On his own land, leaving a child orphaned? No, lads, there's nothing to be gained by shooting me that can't be obtained with a few slaps.'

Number Two is twitching now; impatience reeks off him like steam off fresh dung on a frosty morning behind the cows on their slow walk to the parlour.

'I'll cover you. Get on with it,' he says, producing a sawn-off.

He holds the gun surprisingly still. You were expecting a bad case of nerves, the gun barrel to execute frail, trembling circles in his shaking hands, but he is steady as a rock. He has pointed a gun at a man before.

You stand like a statue as the first blow sinks into your solar plexus. You will not fight back – it is *essential* not to get shot – but you are hard and strong as a bull in his prime; this is not going to be quick. You finally sink to your knees as the blows rain down, one after another. Your eye is closing fast. A concerto of kicks plays out upon your torso, ringing dull in your ears, mingling with the sounds of the men's demands.

They are wary, afraid to put their hands in your pockets. Is it a trap? Are you going to spring back to life from your bloodied mess, like the hero in a B-movie, and turn the tables? You know you are not – you are not acting. You are close to the edge; blackness is creeping in at the sides of your vision. Soon you will be unconscious. You can barely hear yourself now. Your first stoical grunts quickly turned to roars, but now all the sound that is left to you is automatic, each breath thumped out of you, producing its own soft, chordal moan as primal as a baby's sob.

The men stop; you can hear their laboured breathing. It has not been an easy task to fell you, a giant country oak full of knots and sap.

'Alo, there's no call for this. We're not animals. Give us the keys.'

You can scarcely see; you can just about speak: 'I don't think you're animals. You're doing what you think is right. It's in your nature.' You gasp and drag another hacking breath into your burning lungs. 'But I can't give you the tractor to plant your bomb. I just can't. It's not in *my* nature.'

Number Three bends down and kneels on the concrete beside you, a priest's genuflection before the final benediction. In slow motion you see the handgun approach your left temple, lazily whipping you towards blessed oblivion.

You wake in the hospital bed. Cormac is on a plastic chair beside your locker, upon which rests an incongruous bunch of grapes. Your son's face, still innocent of the razor, lights up at your first moan Has it worked? The deception? Is it complete and clean?

You wake again tomorrow; you swim in and out of daylight. Hospital is wonderful, you think, until you notice the spiders. The spiders are coming from behind the wallpaper, from cracks in the lino on the floor of the South Tyrone Hospital. Black-and-orange hairy monsters, they surge from the locker drawer and out of the half-eaten grapes. The spiders swarm over you, making you claw and tear at your skin. The nurses hold you down; they murmur in your ear; they hush your screaming.

'No more morphine,' you beg. 'I'd sooner the pain than the spiders.'

One day the polis come. They toss their hats, with RUC emblazoned, onto your bed. Nurse Josie tut-tuts and removes them. Cormac is to give his evidence in your presence; he has no other guardian. *He came home, he found you in the yard, he called the ambulance. That's it.* He has nothing to add. Neighbour men are taking care of the milking; he is feeding the calves. He is sharing a bedroom with Phelim McNeill. Mrs McNeill is a good cook – *better than you.* All is well. He looks to you for confirmation.

You nod. 'Good man yerself, son.'

Now it's time for your statement. The Royal Ulster Constabulary man turns to a fresh page of his notebook, licks the nib of his biro pensively. At first he makes a few desultory notes, then pauses, incredulous.

'The bull? The bull? You're telling me the bull trampled you? D'you think I came down the fuckin' Bann in a bubble? Someone beat the livin' shite out of you … pardon me, missus.' He blushes and looks quickly at the nurse.

'I've heard worse,' she shrugs. 'I used to be a midwife.'

You struggle to speak more clearly. Every fibre holding your spirit to your body burns with a fiery ache.

'The bull. He turned on me. Quick as can be. It happens. I was lucky to drag meself back til the yard.' You are coarsening your speech, acting the bumpkin. 'He turned on me and the cows panicked. God alone knows how many trampled me. I'm a lucky man.'

'You're a damn fool liar!' The officer's outraged face is puce; a vein throbs in the very centre of his forehead. 'The tractor was in the middle of the shed, the doors near ripped off, the slurry tanker cowped on the floor. We found the keys in a ditch. Explain all that. I'd love ta hear it.'

'I can't explain none of thon, officer. I dunno what I was doing. I daresay I'd lost a bit of blood, had I, Nurse? Mebbe I was trying to drive meself to hospital ...'

'In a tractor? A *tractor* – and a Ford Cortina in the yard with a half-full tank? D'you think that because the uniform's green we're all cabbages? We'll be back, and you can think about obstructing the course of justice while you lie there.'

The door slams back on its hinges, shaking a fine, sparkly film of dust from the top of the lintel onto the shiny, peaked hats as the men stalk out.

Cormac looks at you like you are the second coming of Christ. 'God, Da, that's amazing. You got back from the oak-tree field on your own? That's a-*maz*-ing. Fuckin' Rambo you are.'

He takes your hand and a tear falls down his cheek. Your son is a toddler again, standing at the side of your bed, roused weeping from sleep by a dream of his mammy in heaven. You blink and come back to the present with all its pain and its joy. You have survived; you are here with him. He need not know about, nor fear, the shadows of the men in the masks. Nothing else matters.

'Will we have ta kill the bull now, Da? Now that he's dangerous?'

Your fingers fall weakly from his hand, the joy of holding it outweighed by the pain.

'We won't be killing him. He's no more dangerous than he was last week, and no less. Animals are always dangerous, son. None of us can change what's in our nature.'

Las Vegas in the Hills of Donegal

:::::

'Don't make me go back there' – Cathy's mother twisted round in her seat, glowering furiously – 'or I'll show you the back of my hand.'

'It's not me. It's our Liam,' moaned Cathy. 'His feet are on my part of the seat and he's poking me with his toes.'

'For God's sake, Cathy, he's only a wee fella, half the size of you. How could he be taking up more than his own share of the seat?'

'Can he not go in the front on your knee?'

'I'm not sitting the whole way to Bundoran with a six-year-old child on my knee!' Maeve caught Cathy's eye in the rear-view mirror and gave her the death stare. 'Why can't the pair of youse just sit at peace like Mark?'

Mark smiled angelically and, after his mother turned back to face the road, quietly grabbed a fold of Cathy's belly through her t-shirt and gave it a swift, sharp twist. Cathy rammed her index finger into his ribs, causing him to recoil and whack his head off the car window. They both started to wail simultaneously.

Cathy's father indicated and carefully pulled over to the side of the road.

'What are you doing, Eddie?' asked Maeve.

'I'm doing a three-point turn' – he eased the car smoothly across the road, then slipped it into reverse – 'and then I'm driving home. This shower of ungrateful wee blirts no more deserves a holiday than the man in the moon.'

Soon they were bowling quickly along the road, heading back to Omagh.

'Now look what you've done,' Cathy howled.

'Ach, houl' yer whist, would ya,' whispered Mark. 'He's only bluffing.'

But their father drove all the way back to their terraced house, and he had the car parked and his hand on the door handle before their mother could persuade him to relent.

'Well, go in and make us a cup of tea, seeing as we're here, Maeve love. Then we'll all go to the loo and be back in the car in a quarter of an hour.'

As his wife disappeared through the door of the house, their father turned in his seat and pulled his eyebrows together. Before Cathy and Mark had the sense to shift, he reached in and gave them a good clout round the ear.

'Here's yer choice,' he hissed. 'You can stay here with the McCaffreys, who can't afford a holiday, and eat bread and jam and listen to them Orange bastards parading up and down the town all July, or you can sit like two fuckin' statues all the way from here to Bundoran. But one thing's for sure – me and yer ma is going on our holidays and I don't give one continental damn whether you two wee slabbers comes with us or not.' He glared from one to the other. 'D'you understand?'

Cathy nodded, the tears tripping her. At nearly fourteen, Mark was too old to cry about a clip round the ear, but he nodded too.

'Right, into the loo and straight back in the car afterwards. You too, Mammy's boy.'

Their father pulled Liam out by the wrist and all four walked up to the front door. As Eddie reached out to push the door fully open, he plastered a smile on his face.

'Here we are, love, all friends again. Did you get that tea wet?' He took a long sip from the cup she handed him and smiled as the strain disappeared from her eyes. 'Good woman, just what the doctor ordered.'

'Will I get the kids a cup too?'

'No, love, or they'll all be looking for a toilet and we'll not get there till tomorrow.'

His eyes burnt into Cathy as she slammed her way upstairs to the bathroom. She knew that look, the look that meant a rare paternal explosion had been narrowly avoided, but the fuse was still lit and shortening quickly. She'd want to watch herself.

The journey to Bundoran took less than two hours, even at the snail's pace Maeve favoured, and Eddie glanced into the back seat occasionally where six-year-old Liam was now acting as a buffer between the other two. Their mother had tried to start a sing-song, but the kids hadn't cooperated, so Eddie had slipped a Val Doonican tape into the machine. At least Liam had been happy. Mark mimed slitting his own throat, and Maeve beamed while her precious Liam warbled the song about Paddy McGinty's Goat.

As the car weaved its way along the Boa Island Road, over the small bridges and the blue flashing waters below, Liam sang out in his wobbly small child's voice a song he had certainly not learned from Val Doonican.

'*The sea, oh the sea, is the dum dum dum dee …*'

'What are you on about, you wee eejit?' asked Cathy.

'*Long may it roll …*'

'Oh my God, you are a total simp.'

'*… between England and me …*'

'Seriously, what are you on about?'

'Look,' Liam said, 'we're driving over the sea. Now we're in the Free State.'

'No, we're not, you wee plank,' said Mark, laughing. 'That's not the sea, you stumer, that's Lough Erne.'

'You're so stupid, Liam,' Cathy said. 'How the hell could there be the sea right in the middle of the country like that?'

'Don't call your brother stupid,' shouted their mother. 'He's very bright for his age.'

Mark and Cathy stuck their fingers down their throats and pretended to boke.

'Liam, love,' Maeve continued, 'there's no sea between us and the Free State. It's all the one country.'

'But there is,' Liam said, his voice rising in pitch.

Eddie sighed and waited for one of his son's big hissy fits. In Eddie's opinion, Liam would benefit from the odd toe up the hole. It certainly hadn't done Mark any harm, but Liam was an unexpected late addition to the family, despite the welly boot contraceptives they had always been so careful to use, and Maeve seemed to have placed all her eggs firmly in his basket.

'I see us on the TV every night after Scene Around Six, when the lady sticks the clouds and the rain on the map and there's a big sea all around us,' Liam wailed.

Cathy laughed out loud, and Mark rolled his eyes so far back in his head that Cathy thought they might get stuck there.

'Ach, no wonder the wee pet is confused.' Maeve reached back and rubbed Liam's knee. 'It's just the way they do the weather, love. They only do the six counties. They just leave off the rest of the country, the Free State.'

'It's called the Republic of Ireland,' said Mark haughtily. He had got ninety per cent in his geography exam.

'Them bastards in the BBC would be just as happy if the six counties *were* surrounded by water. It'd suit them down to the ground.'

'Eddie – language!' Maeve looked back at her precious angel, as if his ears might fall off.

'For crying out loud, love, if that's the worst he ever hears, he'll be all right.'

'It's not even the worst he's heard today,' muttered Cathy just low enough that her mother could pretend not to hear.

Silence fell.

The car wended its way towards the border crossing. Every time the speedometer wobbled up towards sixty, Maeve put her hand gently on Eddie's knee and, sighing, he would ease off on the accelerator. Cathy knew her mother had a terror of being stopped by the RUC, and a greater fear yet of the British Army patrols that could appear round any bend. Their da had explained that if the RUC wanted to stop a car, they didn't need the excuse that you were speeding; they could stop you on any notion they took. That didn't seem to reassure their mother.

They all had a good snigger as the road parted company with the shore of Lough Erne and took them through the small town of Leggs.

'All the ones, legs eleven,' roared Cathy like Foghorn Maire who called the bingo on a Friday night.

Her father gave a loud wolf whistle, looked appreciatively over at his wife and put his left hand on her thigh. She swatted his hand away with a happy smile.

'Here we are now, Liam,' said Maeve. 'The border post at Belleek. Once we get on the other side, we'll be in the Free State and you'll see there's no sea between Fermanagh and Donegal.'

'Well, where's the border then? Where's the big wall if there's no sea?'

'It's invisible,' said Cathy. 'It's just a made-up line – all the wealthy bits on our side to make the Brits richer, all the poor bits on the Free State side to learn them a lesson for wanting to be independent.'

'I bet the Brits are wishing they'd never held on to us, now that the Ra is blowing the place to bits,' said Mark staring out the window as the car crawled towards the Irish custom officers and the unarmed gardaí in their old-fashioned serge uniforms, their flat caps like farmers'.

'Whist, now. Not a word till we're on the other side,' Maeve whispered.

The three children fell eerily silent.

'Half the population is heading to the South this year,' grumbled Eddie. 'Did you ever see the like of thon queue?'

'Well, who in their right mind would stay at home this year, and things as bad as they are?' whispered Maeve. 'I wonder will the house be all right, Eddie, or should we have stayed at home this year like the McCaffreys? They'd never burn yer house down and you in it?'

Eddie glanced round at the children.

'Hush, love, we've made our choice. It's only for a fortnight, and if the house burns down, sure we'll all be safe and well, and nothing else matters.'

They well knew that during the worst times, in 1969, the petrol bombs had crashed through the windows of hundreds of homes – empty or full of children, it hadn't made any difference. Now, in the summer of 1981, it still might not make any difference. Better to take the whole family away till the Twelfth was over, and deal with the consequences later.

'Joe McDonnell and Martin Hurson are said to be circling the grave,' Maeve whispered. 'Did you hear anything this morning?'

'They say Hurson won't last much longer, though he's only six weeks on the hunger strike. Sands and the others lasted nine or ten weeks. McDonnell is close to the end.'

'God help their mothers.' Maeve blessed herself. 'God help us all.'

'I don't know, Maeve. Maybe we should head for England. Leave it all behind.'

'England? Are you out of your tiny mind? We'd get some welcome in England at the minute.'

'Well, America then, Canada.'

'Maybe when my mother's gone.'

'Your mother's been dying for five years and still manages to get to the bingo of a Friday and to every whist drive in the county. I wish I was half as sick as she is.'

Cathy interrupted them. 'Wind down yer window, Da. You're wanted.'

The customs official had finally reached their car. He stuck his head through the open window, looked around inside and sighed. His first glance took in the three children, their feet resting on cardboard boxes full of everyday provisions – washing powder, Sunlight washing-up liquid, spaghetti hoops, tomato sauce, Angel Delight.

'We have shops in Donegal you know,' he remarked quietly.

'The price of them! Daylight robbery,' said Maeve scowling.

'It's been a tough year, officer,' Eddie said. 'We were put to the pin of our collar just to gather up the price of the rent of the holiday cottage.' He looked the man straight in the eye and spread out his fingers apologetically. 'Any other year we'd have stayed at home, things is that tight, but this year … well, you know yourself.'

The customs man nodded. 'I know. Come on then. Open the boot and we'll get it over with.'

He made the barest pretence of checking the suitcases and bags of towels, warm sweaters, wellies and raincoats.

'Enjoy your stay in God's own county,' he said at last and waved them through to the Free State, a country so familiar and yet so utterly alien.

Two weeks stretched out ahead of them: Sam Spuds crisps, huge, strange bank notes, cans of Cidona drunk in pubs while they munched scampi and chips out of plastic baskets. Their mother wouldn't be seen dead in a pub at home.

They joined the trail of cars heading into Donegal, brake lights winking and flickering as the drivers negotiated potholes and missing road markings.

'These bloody roads are a disgrace,' muttered Maeve. 'I can feel every filling in my mouth bouncing around.'

'Mammy, what if I get sick? You know I always get sick on Free State roads.'

Maeve handed her back a sturdy plastic bag. 'Keep that open on yer knee and wind down yer window a bit. You won't get sick between here and Bundoran. This is a main road, if you'd believe it!'

Liam had been straining to see out the side windows, even though, sitting in the middle, where Cathy liked to sit, he had a perfect view out the front windscreen.

'I know what's different,' he said. 'Where's all the flags? There's no flags on any of the houses.'

'People down South don't give a tinker's curse for us,' said Mark abruptly. 'That's why there's no flags.'

'Well, you've no business saying that when we haven't even a flag on our own house,' snapped Cathy.

Cathy was disgusted that her mother had refused point-blank to hang a black flag at the front of their house after Bobby Sands died. 'We'll be the only house with no flag,' she had moaned as Hughes, McCreesh and O'Hara died in the weeks that followed. But there were as many homes without flags as had them. Her mother called the owners of the flag-draped homes *a bunch of bloody Provos, bringing down trouble on their own heads*, but Cathy suspected her da would have a flag – if he was let.

'I don't want to upset our Protestant friends,' Maeve had said when Cathy wouldn't let the black-flag issue drop.

'We don't have any Protestant friends.'

'Well, we might – in the future. Things can't go on like this forever.'

'Do you think the Prods are uneasy about whether they upset us or not?' asked Cathy. 'Sure they have their Union Jacks or Paisley flags. And not just this year, but every single year of their lives.'

'Ach, houl' yer whist or I'll show you the back of my hand,' roared Maeve, and Cathy had fled. She didn't really believe her mother would hit her, but there was a first time for everything. Tempers were short in the summer of 1981.

The cottage in Donegal wasn't too bad this year. There were three bedrooms, so Cathy had one of her own. She called her father in to pull back the bedclothes.

'I'm not starting this crack again,' he said, groaning.

'Oh please, Daddy, just today. Just check it for me this one time.'

He ripped back the bedspread with a flourish and loosened up the tightly tucked sheets and blankets.

'All clear.'

Two Julys ago, in a damp, mouldering farmhouse just outside Glenties, her father had had to strip her bed every night and shake out the sheets and blankets in the yard, sending their population of spiders freewheeling into the clammy air. Twenty-four hours later her bed would be repopulated by a new eight-legged community. 'They're the world's first fuckin' homing spiders,' her dad had muttered. 'Should get a bloody prize for finding their way back.'

This year there were no spiders, but the same brown, peaty water flowed from the bathroom tap when Cathy turned it on, and once again there was no twin tub in the kitchen. Her mother would have to wash the clothes by hand, and the whites would bear a faint brown hue for ever more.

'It's not much of a holiday for the wives,' Cathy had overheard her mother say to Mrs McCaffrey, who was afraid to leave home so just pretended she couldn't afford a holiday. 'Same oul' shite, only in some other woman's kitchen, and a big tribe of red-headed kids wandering in and out like they owned the place.'

'They *do* own the place,' Sally McCaffrey had said, laughing.

'You know what I mean. You either rent your house out or you don't. It's not my fault they have to live in a caravan at the bottom of the yard for the month of July. Isn't my money keeping them in the bloody kip for the rest of the year?'

Cathy had crossed her fingers and hoped. Donegal was always better when the holiday house came with a family of girls in a caravan, or in their granny's house across the road – or even in the henhouse, which had happened once. With a team of girls on her side, Cathy could survive the two weeks of rain and boredom, brown water that tasted of soil, and the impatient wait for her wet shoes to dry out beside the stinky turf fire.

As far as Cathy was concerned there was only one bright spot in the whole holiday – the day they went to the amusements. In fact it was the best day of the year – better than the Pope's visit, better even than Christmas. Cathy gave it capital letters in her head: Amusements Day.

Tartan blankets, thermos flasks, bucket and spade at the ready. Sandwiches made and carefully eased back into the waxy paper of the local bakery, which shrieked in red letters, 'Sliced for your convenience! Wrapped for hygiene!' Who in the civilised world had ever heard of unwrapped, unsliced bread, Cathy thought.

Then there was the agony of choosing between the amusements: bumper cars, chair-o-plane, coconut shy, ice cream. Her mother had a weakness for the one-armed bandits. A bright smile played on her face as she tugged the long shiny lever at the side of the machine and set the cylinders racing.

Two cherries and an apple.

Two apples and a banana.

THREE CHERRIES, and the coins tumbling and crashing into the metal dish below.

Her mother whooped and cheered and gave the children fifty pence each from her winnings.

For this one day, Cathy's da silently agreed to refrain from tutting and sighing as her mother fed her store of coins into one machine, unable to leave in case the next player undeservedly won all her money. She was never satisfied until she had won a fortune, or lost every penny she had.

Cathy liked what she called the totter-coin machines. She slid old Free State tuppences, some still bearing the word *florin*, into machines where great teetering mounds of copper coins were heaped up, ready at any moment to tumble into the slot as a swiping arm pushed them seemingly closer to the brink. If those heaps of coppers ever fell off, they never fell into Cathy's hands.

The boys usually spent every penny on bumper cars, until last year when Space Invaders had appeared in the arcade for the first time. Now Mark stood transfixed for hours on end, screaming, and whispering *fuck* hundreds of times, until every penny was gone. There wasn't even a chance of winning it back. Cathy thought Space Invaders was stupid.

This year Cathy's da paid her to take Liam on the bumper cars four times.

Her mother stood at the side shouting, 'They're called dodgems. You're supposed to *avoid* the other cars. He'll be killed!', while Cathy rammed her car into anyone foolish enough to approach her.

'Dodge 'em, my ass,' she whispered to Liam before swearing him to secrecy.

At last, with candy floss in their hair and sand in their underpants, they piled exhausted back into the car. At the holiday home, steaming water, brown as cola, trickled slowly into the huge enamel bath. First Liam, then Cathy, then Mark. Cathy knew that she had her bath before Mark in case she got pregnant from bathing in a boy's water, like a girl at the secondary school had done. Her mother would never allow anything like that to happen to Cathy.

Huddled beside the turf fire drying her hair before bed, she examined the treasures she had won, or grudgingly bought, at the amusements: a pink teddy rabbit eating a carrot, a sliver of Connemara marble with a brown horse statuette attached by ugly gobs of superglue, a goldfish destined to die overnight, poisoned by its last supper of crushed cornflakes.

'The only thing that could have made today better would have been no rain,' said Liam.

'Next year,' said her mother, 'next year, the sun will surely shine.'

'Next year,' said Liam, 'it'll be a scorcher.'

'Next year,' said Cathy, 'we'll spend every single day at the amusements.'

'Next year,' said her father, 'your da will win the football pools.'

One Lucky Bitch

:::::

'Come on you into the toilets with me and hold the door.'

Sonia sighed. 'Can you not just kind of hover and keep it closed with one foot?' she said. 'Sure it mightn't even be broken.'

'Oh for God's sake, of course it's broken.' Cathy tossed her hair and jiggled up and down impatiently. 'There hasn't been a lock on a bog door all the months I've been coming here. Come on, I'm bursting.'

Sonia stepped off the dance floor and the two girls picked their way across the chewing gum-pocked floor of St Cecilia's Hall. In the 1960s, when showbands and céilí bands had packed the hall to bursting, the old parquet had been a thing of beauty. Cathy's mother sometimes spoke of trumpets and saxophones and jiving, sweating couples twirling with skill and flair across that floor.

'I feel sorry for youse uns,' her mother would say. 'We had a lot more fun in my day, and the boys looked after themselves –

clean, and in a shirt and tie. I wouldn't give a curse for any young man these days.' She would cast a glance at her eldest son, face riddled with acne and wearing a torn, faded Pink Floyd T-shirt. 'Yer da was a brilliant dancer.' Then Cathy's da would snort from the armchair and break into a chorus of 'Her eyes they shone like diamonds, I thought her the queen of the land...', and Cathy would mime sticking her fingers down her throat. But it was good to see her ma flushed with pleasure, smiling down at the ironing board or the potato peeler.

Her parents had danced at St Cecilia's Hall in the years before the massacre of the Miami Showband on a dark bend fifty miles away. That shooting had signalled the end of the showband era in Northern Ireland, and the end of the Hall's glory days.

Tonight, under the twirling silver disco-balls, with the bass pulsing through the foundations of the building, Cathy and Sonia didn't notice the scuffed, loosened flooring or think about the history of their parents or of the crumbling hall. They stepped carefully over the puddles of spilled minerals that made the parquet stick to the flimsy soles of their cheap glittery shoes. When they pushed open the heavy doors into the lobby, they gasped in shock at the plummeting temperature and rubbed their bare arms poking out from oversized batwing tops.

The ladies' toilets were even colder.

'Told you it'd be broken,' said Cathy, laughing. 'You stand out there and guard it for me.'

Sonia stood outside the cubicle and shared a cigarette with Gemma McCann. Cathy hated the stink of fags and the way they made her mouth dry and sticky, but what could you do? You didn't want to look like a twelve-year-old at the teenage disco. She stayed in the cubicle until she guessed the stubby butt would be too small to pass to her. Then she smiled at her friends and went straight to the wall of mirrors to fix her lipstick, just in case they felt they had to offer her the last drag.

'Make sure you stub that out properly. And flush it. Don't be letting Father McKeever find butts in here again,' warned an older girl leaning against a sink. 'Jesus, remember the day he found the rubber johnny in the boys' loos?'

All four girls burst out laughing, although none of them had ever seen a condom in real life.

'That's minging. I'd say he had a fit.'

'Sure the whole disco was nearly closed down for good after it. But the hall needs the money, I suppose.'

'That was about a month before I started coming,' said Gemma, slipping her lipstick back into her shirt pocket and twisting the one stained cold-water tap that still worked. 'My da would never let me through the door if he knew about that.'

The girls nodded. Gemma's father, Dominic McCann, was a serious oul' bollox.

'It wasn't used or anything,' the older girl said, laughing and pretending to stick two fingers down her throat. 'Jesus! That'd make you want to boke.'

Cathy and Sonia linked arms and wandered back into the warm enveloping thump and grind of the disco. Flashing neon green and blue lights circled the floor and walls, roamed across clumped hair gel and blue eyeshadow, gaggles of girls in tight PVC miniskirts, and boys in Doc Martens and stone-washed Levis. Madonna's 'Like a Virgin' blared from the speakers as the DJ, fat Tony Malocco who stank of chips and vinegar, bobbed in time to the crowd of swaying, jumping teenagers, oblivious to Father McKeever's flushed cheeks and stare of fury. Cathy thought it was cruel to make Father McKeever supervise the disco every second week when it was obvious that he wanted to drive everyone out with a whip, like Jesus in the temple.

Why couldn't Father O'Donovan do supervisor every week? Father O'Donovan always stayed in the lobby, and only ever went into the disco if there was a ruckus. It's not like he had anything better to do, sitting all night in the big cold parochial house next door.

'Are you dancing?'

Paddy Malone was standing in front of the girls, but they all knew it was Sonia he was talking to.

Sonia wound a strand of her bouncy, naturally curly hair slowly round the forefinger of her right hand and blew a bubble with her gum.

Cathy sighed. Sonia never smelt of perming lotion, and never had three or four inches of suspiciously straight hair at the crown of her head before the poodle-tight curls started. Unlike Cathy. It was a bloody good job that Sonia was such a laugh and never held a grudge. It was a bloody good job she never told your secrets to anyone, didn't even write them on the condensation of the school bus window on a wet morning, *Cathy loves Mickey Murphy TID* – True If Destroyed. It was just as bloody well that Sonia never did any of those things, for she was good-looking enough to get herself a few enemies. But Sonia had no enemies, everyone loved her. She was one lucky bitch.

'Who are you asking for?' Sonia eventually said.

'Donal Farrell. He's over there, beside that pillar.'

'I know who Donal Farrell is, ya big tool.'

'I'd say she does,' said Cathy, laughing. 'Who wouldn't know Donal Farrell?'

It was a relief to hear Farrell's name; he was way out of Cathy's league. If Farrell and Sonia snogged away in a dark corner for the rest of the night – the rest of the *year*, for that matter – it wouldn't affect Cathy's chances of getting a boy one bit. She'd be glad to see Sonia out of the way, happy, with a boy Cathy had no chance in hell of getting for herself. She knew she wasn't bad-looking – her perm was new, her lipstick fresh – but she was sick of being left with the depleted group of girls who bounced and bopped defiantly through the final thirty minutes every week, pretending to have the time of their lives after the slow set had cleared all the newly established couples into the seats.

Cathy waved goodbye to her friend, a tiny gesture that meant, *Keep one eye on me, I'll rescue you if you need me*, but neither of them had ever heard that Farrell was a wandering-hands-pig, and those things spread quickly enough.

Paddy Malone led Sonia across the hall, swatting aside bouncing bodies, which ricocheted wildly off into the flashing, pulsating crowd.

Sonia stood in front of Donal Farrell and they chewed their gum silently for a moment, wondering where to start.

'D'ya wanna dance?'

Everyone knew that 'Like a Virgin' was Chipper Tony's signal that any minute now the huffing and puffing of 'Je t'aime' would drift across the floor and Father McKeever would disappear for the carefully measured fifteen minutes of the slow set. You had to be careful towards the end – ready and decent – for the priest wouldn't think twice about bounding onto the stage and lifting the stylus from the record if it carried on into a sixteenth or seventeenth minute.

'No,' said Sonia. 'Sit down here beside me.'

An entire Thursday night cinema's-worth of seating had been pushed well back against the wall under the balcony. A small cloud of dust rose up from the stained red-velvet plush of a double love-seat as they plumped down.

Donal spat his chewing gum onto the floor; Sonia popped hers back into its silver paper to keep for later. Then they turned to each other. They banged noses, laughed, glanced around to check that no one had spotted their awkward start, but managed to connect lips on the second attempt.

'Donal, this isn't really my kinda thing,' Sonia said a few minutes later.

'What? I haven't done nothing – didn't even slip the hand.'

'Jesus, no, and don't bother trying it.' A blush spread over Sonia's face. 'I just mean I never really fancy snogging in here, where everyone can see.'

'Will we go outside?'

'Yeah, but I'm serious. I'm going out because I don't want people gawking at me with your tongue in my face, not because I want to do anything we can't do in here.'

'Get your coat.'

Sonia caught Cathy's eye and mimed putting on her coat. 'Je t'aime' was nearly over and the dance floor was full of gyrating, undulating couples. Eilish Toner was discreetly wriggling in Paddy Malone's grip, trying to slide down a little so Paddy's hand would land back up on her waist from its current location on the curve of her ass. It seemed to be a losing battle.

Most of the still unattached had given up hope and were leaning against the mineral bar, sucking Cokes through straws and eating cheese and onion crisps. It was time for Cathy to join them. Cathy gave Sonia a tiny, subtle thumbs up and watched wistfully as her friend walked out to the lobby with the only properly good-looking boy in the whole of St Cecilia's Hall. That's one lucky bitch, Cathy thought to herself.

And that's exactly how Sonia's mother would describe her daughter for years afterwards.

'She was one lucky bitch, I'm telling you. Her and Donal, the pair of them. The peelers found them round the back an hour later, huddled on the cellar steps, frozen to the spot, gripping on to one another for dear life. I'd been screaming her name for forty minutes from behind the police tape at the gates of the car park. We couldn't get one word out of either of them for hours. Thought they'd been struck dumb.'

Sonia's mother would pause for dramatic effect and bless herself at this point every time she told the story. Sonia, though, would look at the ground and clench her teeth and wish her mother would shut the fuck up, or drop dead. Still making a holy show of her, all these years later, when any normal person just wanted to forget.

'The pair of them never seen a thing, although they heard it all,' her mother would go on. 'Heard the car screech up, the shouting, the gunfire, everything. They were near enough the only kids who didn't come out in a bag or covered in someone else's blood, the night they shot up St Cecilia's Hall. She was one lucky bitch.'

A Sliver of the Moon

::::::

'Ah for fuck's sake.'

I slam my hand down on the steering wheel. Through the condensation weeping down the inside of the windscreen and the wipers flailing ineffectually at the tempest outside, I can just about discern the dark, motionless hulk lying in the long grass of the verge to my left.

'Useless bastards,' I mutter. 'Throughother useless carns. Who else in the whole world would leave their dog out in weather like this except Felix Campbell?'

There isn't the slightest flicker of movement from the corpse. I have pulled to a halt right outside Campbell's gateway, but it's a quarter mile up the long lane to their farmhouse. Nobody would know if I simply drove on and left them to find their old half-blind black Labrador in the morning.

'Hutch,' I say suddenly in the quiet cockpit of the car, my words punctuated only by the flapping of the wiper blades. 'This one's called Hutch. Starsky's been dead these years past, since the co-op milk tanker drove over him. And now I've driven over the other. Fucking stupid names. And fucking stupid wanker Felix Campbell to leave the poor oul' divil out in the bucketing rain.'

So this is the thanks a poor widow-man gets for heading out to the Friday evening devotions on a wild night like this, instead of staying warm by the fire and watching Cormac do his homework. Thanks a lot, God.

What if the dog isn't full dead yet? What if the useless, faithful oul' cur is lying there, spine broken, mouth agape in agony, lying stock-still but sensible? What if it has damaged my new Vauxhall, barely twenty thousand mile on her and never once used to transport a sick calf or bales of hay? It would have been a fairly uneven battle between soft, yielding body and shiny, steel bumper, but still ...

Fuck it to hell and back, I'm going to have to step out into the worst of a March night and check the car over, although the only way to get the Campbells to pay for any damage would be to take them through the court. Felix Campbell is as tight as a duck's arse, and that's watertight. While I'm out there, I'll check the oul' dog too, and whack his brains out with the wheel brace if he looks truly and utterly fucked. It's the least I can do.

I pull my hood up over my head. Luckily the waterproof trousers are already concertinaed round the legs of my wellies in the footwell of the passenger seat. I flick on the hazard lights and gasp as a sudden icy attack of rain squalls in through the opened door. It's as cold as charity out there tonight.

By the light of my powerful torch the car seems okay so far; I'll check properly in the morning. As I approach the dog, the light executes wavering arcs through the teeming rain. It is a strange long thin shape, this old dog. I must have made mincemeat out of it.

The rainwater is hammering down like the wrath of God as

I reach the still, silent shape. I can just make out two arms, two legs and a pale circle of face under a black woollen cap. From the skid marks and the thick rut that my left front wheel has churned out of the clabber of the saturated verge, I can see that the car has struck the body half-on and half-off the roadway, and that the poor crather was long dead before ever I turned the corner at Campbell's boundary hedge. Unless he bound his own hands and feet and slapped a wedge of duct tape across his own mouth before flinging himself into my path.

'Shit. Shit. What the fuck did I ever do to deserve this?'

The words spring out of my mouth before I can stop them, and the shame rises up thick and fast behind them. Thank God Cormac isn't here to hear them, nor a sinner else neither. All things considered, I'd rather find a murder victim than be one. There's no help for it – I'll have to get the peelers. Usually I try to give the RUC a wide berth, if at all possible. Who wouldn't?

Will I push the poor fucker back onto the verge? What are the chances that another car will drive along this godforsaken country lane in the few minutes it'll take me to rouse the Campbells, and leave yet another set of wheel-tracks on this poor divil?

I don't move him in the end, though I hum and haw about it for a minute or two. Since Bid went under the ground, Cormac only has the one parent, and I won't be much use to him if I lose a leg, or get kilt altogether. If the corpse had been booby-trapped, chances are the clout of the car would have detonated it already, but I'll not take the gamble. The RUC sometimes call Anthony to the side of a road like this, and then he and Doctor McKenna have a fierce, furious row about which of them will touch the sadly departed first, while the cops hang back in their armoured personnel carriers. Anthony usually wins for, as he says, there's no point administering the last rites to a body if the doctor hasn't told you yet whether it lives or not. 'If he's still hanging on by a thread,' says Anthony, 'he needs a doctor more than a priest, and if he's already dead, he's not going to get any deader whether he gets the oil of chrism right now or in ten minutes' time.' I'd say McKenna hates our Anthony's fucking guts.

Hutch sets up a ferocious racket when I bang on Felix's door; blind the old dog might be, but there's nothing wrong with his ears, or his bark. I can imagine the commotion inside: Veronica Campbell glancing across at her husband and trying to act calm for the childer. I pity Veronica's pounding pulse and the sick plunging in her gut, for Christ knows, no casual caller would be popping in on a night like this for a cup of tea or to ask Felix for help with a tight calving, not without phoning first.

There's no point in me shouting my name, for the wind would whip the voice from a banshee tonight. There hasn't been a farmer shot round these parts for a good few years, not since Andy Mackle, but the memory of that is only lightly buried. If I were the man shuffling slowly to open the back door to a stranger on a dirty night like this, I'd be shitting myself. And Cormac would be well hid under the bed, whether he liked it or not.

I swear to God I can see the tears of relief in Felix Campbell's eyes when he recognises me and pulls me in to drip on the worn lino of the scullery.

I phone Cormac first and tell him I'm delayed, to take a couple of cuts of bread and butter and go to bed at nine o clock. 'And don't be touching the kettle, or burning the house down round yerself,' I add, just for the pleasure of hearing his derisive snort and imagining him tossing his eyes up to heaven.

When the police Land Rover pulls up, Felix and I are at opposite ends of the body with our torches. But we needn't have feared – there hasn't been another car along since I clipped it. If I hadn't gone out to the bloody stupid devotions, like all the oul' biddies *licking the altar railings*, as Anthony calls it, the dead man would have lain all night in the rain. In that case, I suppose, whatever chance there was of finding evidence would have been well and truly gone. If I ever get the opportunity, I'm going to stick my boot into Felix's Labrador. If I hadn't been so soft and fearing to leave him suffer, I could be home in my armchair, playing Scrabble with Cormac and not having to pretend to let him win.

'Evening officer,' I say, all polite and extra helpful. 'Sorry to get you out on a night like this. A bad state of affairs.'

He nods quickly.

Christ, they've sent out a youngster. He's half my age at a stretch.

Campbell says nothing, which is often the wisest course of action. The polisman heads over to the corpse and I wonder if he will shudder or blanch, or even turn away and vomit, but his face barely registers any change and he walks calmly away, as if executed bodies turn up on his watch every day. Of course, I can tell at a glance that this RUC man is as Black as yer boot, wee Orange face on him, and thon poor divil on the grass is almost certainly Catholic; probably fallen on the wrong side of one of his own brigade, or been turned by the Brits, blackmailed into squealing on his friends and comrades. It happens. And it never ends well.

I'm settling in for the long haul; I've given up any notion of seeing my bed this side of midnight, but the peeler just jots down my name, address and phone number, has a quick peep at the driving licence to make sure I'm telling the truth and then sends me and Felix home.

'We could be here all night waiting for forensics,' he says, 'for all the good that'll do us on a night like this. Ye might as well get on home afore we close the road.'

Me and Felix doesn't have to be told twice.

I make a terrible clatter when I come into the scullery, taking twice as long as I usually do to pull off the soaking raincoat and the waterproof trousers. A puddle gathers on the newly tiled blue and white floor as the water pours out of the rubberised folds of the fabric. I toss an old tea towel down on top of it like Mary-Ann does – Bid'll be turning in her grave – and then I thump slowly up the stairs to Cormac's room, where the light that was shining behind the curtains as I pulled into the yard has since been quenched. I slip a hand under the blankets, and right enough the sheet below them is as cold as a witch's tit. I'd say he's been in bed for about three minutes, the wee skite, and it's well past eleven o'clock. There's a new-built Lego farmhouse laid out on the floor where there never was one before. I'm not great at the amateur dramatics myself, but the snores of Cormac wouldn't convince a deaf man.

I slide down onto the floor beside the bed and rest my hand ever so gently on the crown of his head, the calluses snagging and catching in his hair.

'Fast asleep. Wee pet. The best wee boy in Ireland. I wonder do you know how much I love you?'

I'm laying it on a bit thick, but when will I get another chance to say these things?

'Do you know that when I look at you, I see all the little that's good about me and everything that was good about your mother all wrapped up in one perfect person?'

The fake snoring has stopped now; the breathing is more natural.

'How could you know what I'd do for you? I wish you could have the whole world. There's nothing I wouldn't do to keep my wee man safe.'

I think about the young lad dead on the verge, hands bound, and the endless, howling Gethsemane that awaits his father tomorrow when the polis knock on the door. Please God, he's too young to have a wife and family of his own. How this tortured corner of a bitter country eats her young, like a bad bitch of a sow that turns in the farrowing pen and devours the banbh at her own breast.

My hand, coarse as Grade 60 sandpaper, gently caresses my boy's hair.

'There's nothing I'd deny you. I'd sell the good farm of land my father's father chose for you and take you to the ends of the world to keep you out of trouble.'

I have thought of this before; we could head to the wide open plains of Alberta, or to the bone-dry outback of Western Australia. We wouldn't be the first, nor the last.

The child shifts, barely perceptibly, under my hand.

'I'd give you anything you asked for. I wish you all the wealth of the wide world and the peace of long quiet nights, and hope that your every dream will come true beyond your wildest imaginings. There is nothing you can ask of me that I would not willingly give.'

'Dad?' The smirking face pops out, eyes wide, no pretence of a gradual rousing from slumber. 'Dad, do you really mean all that oul' shite?'

'Every word of it, Cormac. There's nothing you can ask for that I wouldn't happily give.'

'Can I have a bag of Tayto and one of the crème eggs you've hidden in the top shelf of the larder?'

'Quit acting the maggot. It's midnight – and it's Lent.'

'But you said there was nothing I couldn't ask for.'

'Yer daddy says more than his prayers.'

Cormac snuggles back under the blankets and I go downstairs and out into the calving shed for a last check on the springing heifers. The warm sweet smell of hay and of manure in day-old straw greets me at the door. This place is in my blood, in the marrow of my bones; the care of the hedges and boundaries and animals is closer to love than to duty. But I would leave it all behind, without a glance or a tear, if any mad Fenian bastard tried to put a gun in my son's hand and make another martyr for the motherland.

All is well with the heifers.

I pause to use the door scraper before entering the house. The storm has passed. A sliver of equinoctial moon shines on the yard – and on the dead boy a few miles away, and on the polis who guard him; the polis at whom, on another day, he might have shot, or they at him. I bolt the door behind me.

The choice is whiskey or tea. It's a close-run thing but in the end I wet the tea. I'll face whatever news tomorrow brings with a clear head.

J-1

::::::

Gemma McCann opened the door of Room 356 and sighed. The reek of stale cigarettes and spilled drink poured out into the hotel hallway and she felt last night's combination of French fries, Boston cream doughnuts and Mickey's Big Mouth beer churn uneasily in her guts.

She wedged the housekeeping cart across the open doorway, so that Miss Jennifer could glance in as she passed by on her inspection round, and started picking the discarded bed linen off the floor.

The other chambermaids turned on the televisions as they worked, timing quiet chores with their favourite soaps, and hoovering during the ads, but Gemma didn't watch American TV. It was all shite.

She bent down to grab the bedspread off the carpet and felt her head spin. She sank onto the bed and moaned quietly. She was never touching alcohol again.

But she loved the way condensation gathered on the green glass as she pulled a big 40 oz. bottle of Mickey's from the huge fridge in the liquor store; the beer would be warm by the time she reached the bottom. Gemma's new American friends didn't know why she thought Mickey's Big Mouth was so hilarious. Americans didn't know that 'mickey' is another word for, you know …

Gemma's new American friends didn't drink Mickey's. They said it was for poor white trash. They said it was for scumbags. They said it was rotgut and she should drink Sam Adams, like them. But half as much Sam Adams cost twice as much money and Gemma was saving every penny.

Well, not every penny, she conceded, but close enough.

Room 356 was not going to clean itself, so she struggled back up off the bed, moving her head as little as she could, and waited for the tiny, flashing lights in front of her eyes to die away. Miss Jennifer had given her the evil eye when she'd crawled into the staffroom that morning to collect her room-list. Three checkouts and ten staying-ons. Staying-ons were a right pain in the hole – twice as much work as a checkout.

'You gotta problem, honey?' Miss Jennifer asked. 'You rather lay on the beach today?'

Gemma smiled. 'Sure would, Miss J,' she'd said, but the effort of pretending was too much and she slunk out to collect her cleaning cart.

'Jesus, God-a-mighty, girl,' said Amber as they queued outside the supplies station, 'did you sleep in those clothes?'

'Is it that bad?'

'You stink, Irish girl. Every breath you take. Keep your stinky liquor breath off me.'

'I had a shower and the clothes are clean.'

'Girl, it's leaking outta yore pores then.' Amber put her hands on her hips and stood back, biting her lip. 'Are you taking care of yourself? Are you being careful?'

Gemma blushed and lowered her voice to a whisper. 'What do you mean, like … sex?'

'Yes, I mean like sex. If you're not careful you're gonna end up like me.'

::::::

Miss Jennifer had a low opinion of Gemma's choice in friends. When she saw that Amber and Gemma were spending too many lunch breaks together she called Gemma into the office.

'Why don't you eat your lunch with Nicola, honey?' she said. 'Nicola's from Ireland too. I think Nicola is lonely for a face from home.'

'Nicola's from Scotland.'

'Well, that's what I meant. That Nicola is a nice girl, like you. She's at college, like you. Maybe you should pay that Amber girl a bit more never-you-mind, huh?'

::::::

Amber was poor white trash – she said so herself. She lived in a town ten miles inland and came to the coast each day in a car so bockety she wasn't allowed to park in the hotel parking lot. Amber had dropped out of high school. Amber had a five-year contraceptive implant in her left arm.

She'd been working with Gemma on the first day, showing her the ropes, teaching her the little tricks ('If the taps and mirrors are shining, the bathroom's clean, honey, clean enough, leastways') when she'd banged her arm on the door jamb and cursed. That was a black mark against Amber for her potty-mouth. Gemma laughed the first time Miss Jennifer warned her about potty-mouth talk, but she hadn't been joking. Americans don't swear.

123

And they don't give financial assistance to struggling unmarried mothers, not unless they get the five-year contraceptive implant.

'You're fucking joking me?' Gemma exclaimed. 'You can't be fucking serious. They can't do that. They can't tell you what to do with your own body.'

'You're right,' Amber said, rubbing the spot where the tiny scar of the implantation was already fading on her lean, tanned arm. 'They can't make me. This is the land of the free. 'Course I can say no. Long as I don't mind starving to death, and little Janine with me.' She had reached over and billowed out a fresh white sheet, flipping the opposite hems expertly towards Gemma's side of the huge bed. 'Why, what happens to teen moms in your part of the world?'

'Well, it's the nineties, for God's sake. I don't know what they do, but they don't get blackmailed into irreversible medical treatment. They stay at home with their mothers, I suppose, until they get back on their feet.'

'So that's what you'd do? Stay at home with your mother?'

'Oh, Jesus, no. My mother would fucking kill me. She's dead set on me being a secondary school teacher after college. My father — he'd kill both of us, me and the boy.'

'So what would you do? You never had a bit of a scare? You never went two, three days late and thought, well here goes?'

Gemma shook her head and blushed. 'I've never done it.'

'Say what?' Amber dropped the bedspread. 'What the hell age are you girl?'

'I'm nearly nineteen.'

'Nineteen.' Amber stared at her and started to laugh. 'Are you Amish?'

'I don't think so.'

'Honey, you'd know if you were Amish. How the hell you get to be a nineteen-year-old virgin? It must be religion, right?'

Gemma ran through a list in her head of the girls she lived with in Queen's University Halls – Noeleen, Cathy, Patricia, Sonia, all girls she had come through seven years at Loreto College convent with. She was safe enough there. No way would they have done it and not told her. Louise? Louise was Presbyterian – didn't even drink, never mind have sex, and definitely disapproved of Gemma and her hard-drinking Fenian friends. Maybe Laura? Laura and Matthew had been going steady since Upper Sixth. Maybe Laura.

'I don't think any of my friends have done it yet—'

'Well, I'll be damned. Tuck in that corner properly. Your side's a mess.' Amber smoothed the coverlet, satisfied at last. 'What about the boys?'

'What about them?'

'Well, excuse me! What about them? Aren't they at you every moment of the day, trying to wear you down?'

'Good luck to them. What's he going to do about it, your own boyfriend, like? Hold you down and rape you?' Gemma laughed loudly.

Amber shook her head and sighed. 'Honey, you're a lamb to the slaughter.'

:::::

The carpet in Room 356 wasn't too bad, Gemma didn't bother moving the heavy armchairs and table out of the way; she just hoovered around them. There was a used condom in the bathroom, but Gemma was cool with that now. She just slipped on her gloves and changed the bin liner. It's not as if they had left it on the bedroom floor like some of the mingers in other rooms she had cleaned.

She had taken to carrying a condom in her purse, tucked in beside the dollar bill tips from the evening job at Ray's Diner. It was the only way she could get Amber off her case. Every day at 4 p.m. Amber jumped back into her jalopy and rattled off to baby Janine – 'the cutest thing you ever did see' – and every day, as they parted at the staff entrance, Amber would put her hand on Gemma's arm and say, 'You be careful now.'

So Gemma had bought a condom from a dispenser in the bathroom at Marty's bar, a dive where the worst photocopy of someone else's passport served as adequate ID, and she slipped it into her purse beside her fake USIT travel card and her fake student card. The condom felt like the biggest fake of all. It wasn't as if she was ever going to need it.

She paused on the threshold of Room 356 and ticked her room-list. One down, twelve to go, if she didn't boke on the carpet of the hallway first.

Imagine having morning sickness, she thought to herself as the floor swayed under her feet and a bead of sweat trickled down her cheek. Imagine feeling like this every day for months and not even the pleasure of getting drunk first. The spasm passed and she grabbed the handles of the housekeeping cart. *Getting pregnant – Christ!* Could there be anything worse? Gemma thought of the condom in her purse, her shield against all harm. She would never, ever in her life have sex without one, not until she was safely married anyway. Social suicide. Gemma had a lot more drinking and dancing to do before tying the noose of motherhood round her neck.

Miss Jennifer passed her in the corridor and sniffed.

The Widow's Mite

:::::

I never had any money for the black babies. Every day I'd watch the other girls – not all of them, just the same select few – strut up to Sister Oliver's table and slip their coins into the mission box.

'Any more money for the poor black babies, or are you all too greedy spending it in the tuckshop?'

I'd sit on my hands and look at the wooden desktop, scribbled all over with hundreds of girls' names, or fiddle with the empty china inkwell. I never had even one penny for the black babies. You'd think you'd get used to something like that, wouldn't you, something that happens every day, something that doesn't hurt a body, but I never did.

I tried not to look at the pictures on the box. On one side was a fat, round, inky black baby, as glossy as a freshly polished boot, and on the other side, a dusty collection of bones with skin stretched across and eyes with barely a hint of life in them. All a body needed to do to magic one wee child into the other was feed the insatiable plastic box.

'Good girl, Sonia,' Sister Oliver would say as a coin slid down with a dull chink into the bowels of the box. 'Good girl, Cathy.'

Noeleen Bradley always gave her hair a little swish as she turned back from the teacher's table and I never understood why, for there were no boys in the class to notice her shining ringlets or the first swell of her tits against the black pinafore. You might think she swished it just to annoy me, but in truth I wasn't that important.

The day after my tenth birthday I hoisted myself up from behind the desk designed for a smaller, more girly girl.

Twenty tiny, bird-pecked bottles of milk were lined up and carefully balanced on the heating pipe to defrost. I held my breath and sucked in my gut as I squeezed past them.

'Watch out, for heaven's sake, you clumsy lummox,' said Sister Oliver. 'If you break them, you'll clean it up after you,' she added.

Nineteen pairs of eyes followed me as I inched past the radiator and moved to the teacher's table. I knew what they all thought about me. I'm not deaf or stupid, although I might look it. I know I look like I haven't the wit would take me in out of the rain – always have, always will. But just because I preferred being alone in the rain with my hood pulled up to being stuck under the playground shelter with them doesn't mean I'm as green as I'm cabbage-looking.

Noeleen dropped her coin into the slot and tossed her hair out of her eyes, watching me make a holy show of myself in front of the class. If it wasn't the first time I'd donated, I certainly couldn't remember the last time.

Our pinafores had a pocket just below the red sash-girdle, tucked into the shapeless pleats that were never ironed properly. For once, my pocket had more in it than a holey well-used snot-rag.

'Where did you get that money?' Sister Oliver asked.

'I got it for my birthday, Sister. Yesterday was my birthday.'

She might have known that – it must have been written down somewhere – but the girls wouldn't have, for I'd brought no cake nor butterfly buns to school to share, not this year, not ever.

'Don't be ridiculous.' Sister Oliver grabbed my arm, eyes blinking furiously under her veil. 'A pound note? Who'd give you a pound note?'

'Mrs Aitchison.'

'Who on earth is Mrs Aitchison?'

'She works in the kitchens. She's not a nun. She's got children of her own. I help her to peel the spuds.'

The Good Faith House nuns were different from the school nuns, you see – they wore long white gowns like angels, not like Sister Oliver's drab black knee-length skirt. They didn't act like angels though. An angel would put her arms round you. An angel would wrap her giant white wings round you, like in the picture of the little girl straying too close to the riverbank that hung in the assembly hall. The Good Faith nuns just counted me and checked me the odd time for head lice; Sister Oliver gave me pictures to colour instead of doing workbooks; everything else was Mrs Aitchison.

Sister Oliver's fingers cut deep into my right arm, even through the red jumper and the greying sleeve of my white school blouse. I knew I'd find five little bruises the morrow. I didn't bruise very often, for no one ever touched me or pushed me, or tripped me over during games. *Don't take milk from Sarah Brady*, the girls whispered every day when the two milk-girls were chosen. *Don't touch the ball after Sarah Brady. She's got germs.*

I didn't mean to whimper; the noise just came out of me. Sister Oliver dropped my arm like she'd been bitten by a cleg. I don't think she meant to wipe her hand on her skirt; those are just the things people do sometimes. Nowadays, when anyone touches me, they have plastic gloves on and take care not to mark me. Still no arms around me, though, still no enveloping wings.

'Tell the truth and shame the devil.'

'I *am* telling the truth, Sister. Mrs Aitchison found out it was my birthday.'

'You're telling me that Mrs Aitchison works in the kitchen of the Good Faith House?'

And then I knew why it sounded so strange. No wonder Sister Oliver didn't believe me.

'Oh it's alright. I know what it sounds like, but she's a Devlin by birth, and her husband turned just before they were married.' Mrs Aitchison had told me that herself, half-ashamed of the Proddy surname and half proud of saving her husband's immortal soul. 'She said that now I'm old and in double numbers she'd give me 50p, but she gave me a pound.'

'And you're giving it to the black babies?'

'Yes, Sister.'

'Do I look stupid to you? Do I look like I came down from heaven in the last shower?'

'No.'

'No, what?' Sister Oliver's face was as red as a brick under her face powder and her breath was coming fast.

'No, *Sister*.'

'Put the money on the desk.'

'But it's for the black babies.'

'Put it on the desk till I get to the bottom of this.'

She wrenched my fingers open and the banknote floated down, landing Queen's face up on the pile of open copybooks. I longed to reach out and grab it, but as I said before, I'm not as thick as I look. Instead, I pulled my fat plait of mousey brown hair round with my left hand and stuck it in my mouth for a good chew. I'd long since started eating everything that wasn't nailed down – the scraps off other Good Faith plates, apple cores out of the bins, tissues (clean or used) and, when all else failed, my own split ends. I should have spent the pound note in the tuckshop. That's what every sinew of my fat, disgusting body had called out for me to do.

'Go and sit down.'

'But –'

'Sit down! As if you, above anyone in this class, are going to have a pound note to put in the collection box.'

'But –' I swayed and grabbed the table for support. For the very first time I was aware of the pounding of my heart as it laboured to pump blood around its faulty valves. 'It's the widow's mite.'

'What?'

'The widow's mite, like in the bible.' I turned and stared at Noeleen who, every day after dropping her 10p in the black babies' box, spent the same amount in the tuckshop. *'They have contributed from their surplus, but she has given all she had.'*

Noeleen took a quare gunk at me. She could tell I was having a dig but she wasn't sure exactly how.

'I'll phone Sister Marguerite at lunchtime. You better hope she confirms your story.'

No one caught my eye as I waddled back to my seat – there was no grimace of sympathy, no promise of consolation at the lunch break. I would eat my potatoes and gravy in silence at the Primary Six table as I did every day. *Don't ask Sarah Brady to pass the salt. Don't let her touch the water jug.*

If Sister Oliver ever got to the bottom of the mystery of the pound note, she never told me, and I never got to fold the crisp thick paper and slip it through the slot of the collection box. I told

Mrs Aitchison I spent it on Blackjacks and Fruit Salads and shared them with my friends, Cathy and Sonia and Noeleen, until our tongues were rainbow-hued. 'Good girl,' she'd whispered. 'It's nice to share with the other wee girls.' And I went back to peeling the spuds while she stirred arrowroot into the bubbling rhubarb until it was as thick as jam.

I wasn't the only girl in the Good Faith, of course. There were all types of us – mongols, spastics, a few girls with a wee *want* in them, 'simps' we called them but they're called something else now. Some of them were nice enough, but no use at all to Mrs Aitchison.

None of them other girls ever went to school, 'which is just as well,' says I to Mrs Aitchison, 'for Noeleen says her mother says it's bad enough having a wee bastard like me in the class.'

Mrs Aitchison sniffed.

'Thon boul' wee strap has no business talking to you about things like that. And anyway, it's nathin' to do with you. Sure the blame is all your mother's.'

'And my father's too, I suppose?'

'Hmm.'

After that, Agnes Aitchison never forgot my birthday, and when I left the Good Faith House for the last time I had eight pound notes in my pocket and the phone number for the unemployment bureau to sort me out with the brew. Twenty-five pound a week and my rent paid, it was at the time, and it seemed a fierce amount to me at first.

It didn't take me long to find new things to eat. Crisps, chocolate, cake, ice cream. I never did try a Blackjack though, or a Fruit Salad, although they looked nice in their waxed paper. When I had a really bad day, and that was often enough, I'd try something new – orange peel, banana skin, chalk, a rubber off the top of a HB pencil when I got a job in the bookies office, tiny bits of broken glass. I thought I would die for sure the first time I wrapped a flake of glass in a slice of thickly buttered bread. But I didn't. It didn't seem to do me any harm at all.

I put my hand on a bottle of weedkiller once in McNicholl's hardware, you know, but I didn't buy it in the end. I guess I supposed my life wasn't bad enough to check out of it just yet. I bought some daffodil bulbs instead and had a nibble. That was one of the worst experiments, to be honest – worse by far than the broken glass days – spent it boking my ring up all round me.

I suppose it's not too much of a surprise that the heart packed in. You wouldn't think it to look at me now, but the size of me in those days! Beef to the heels like a Mullingar heifer. Even the old-woman knickers in Dunnes Stores hardly covered me. Who was to know about the leaking valves? It's not like Mrs Aitchison was a doctor or nothing, and although she said the sound of me breathing got on her wick, I just tried to close my mouth and drag the air in through my nose. *Well, pardon me for breathing*, Cathy and Sonia and the other girls at school used to say. I just thought that no parents could bear the sound of their children heaving air into their lungs. Not that Mrs Aitchison was my parent, or my guardian angel for that matter, but you know what I mean.

I've lost that much weight you could pick me up and carry me around for the day, if the mood took you. And if you did, I'd lean my head into your strong, man-smelling shoulder and pretend you were giving me a hug. But the lifts in this hospital are big enough to wheel the bed right in, if I need to go anywhere, and that's a rarity.

Did you not know about the black babies? I'm starting to think you didn't, and you looking at the ground while I tell you the story. It's nothing to be ashamed of, for either of us. We all knew it was the English who went over there and made a complete fucking

Horlicks of the place, just like they done here. Sure, we were kindred spirits, the Irish and the darkies, that's what we were told. Every Christmas when the BBC showed *Zulu Dawn*, all the wee taigs in Northern Ireland were rooting for the darkies to come up over thon hill and stamp the English army into the ground. I seen it myself, years later – a bloody good film it is too.

Did you really not know that we were dropping our pennies and 10p coins into plastic boxes for you? We were all mad for the black babies, me and Noeleen and Sister Oliver – every Catholic school in Ireland. But you weren't supposed to take it as an invitation. We were happy to send you our money and our old winter coats and our worn out boots, but youse weren't supposed to turn up here and *take our jobs* and build your shouty-clappy churches – half of youse are no more Catholic than wee Sammy Wilson, and after all we done for you. Youse weren't supposed to come here and walk around with your big white teeth and your secret languages that the patients can't make head nor tail of. No, that wasn't part of the plan at all.

But I'm glad you're here, if that makes any difference. I like to lie here in bed with the rails up and the little oxygen prongs settled just rightly under my nose and look at you. I like to think of Sister Oliver and Sister Marguerite and how they would have a lock of fits each if they knew I was being lifted and laid by a kind, gentle, black Protestant man. You don't know why I'm laughing. That's because you don't know that when I was a child a Black man was a white man or an Orange one, and the only darkies we ever seen wore British Army uniforms and lay in the ditches with the muzzles of their rifles poking out.

A long time ago? God love you, not at all. Sure you're older than I am, I'd say. I'm talking 1980 here – a year after the Pope came and I was the only girl in the class didn't get to take my John Paul II scrapbook home to my ma and tell her how he loved all the children of the world. *Young people of Ireland, I luff you*, he said, but there was no TV in the Good Faith House, so I never knew he loved me until it was too late.

A heart transplant? Ach, God love you in your innocence. There'll be no spare heart wasted on me who hasn't had a visitor in the six months I've been attached to yon machine.

I know you need to get on. I won't hold you back any longer from your work. I just wanted you to know I wish I'd managed to get that pound note into the collection box. It boils my pish to lie here and think thon bitch Noeleen Bradley done more for the black babies than I'll ever do.

I'll lie here and think about the widow's mite, and when you get to church on Sunday, would you ask the Protestant Jesus for me would the widow not have been better off keeping her coin for herself. I think she might, so she might.

Breathing

:::::

'Get up outta that, Alo! Get up and come with me now. The calf is dying.' A gust of wind ripped the farmhouse door from Gemma's hands and slammed it backwards on its complaining hinges. 'And I think the vet might be heading the same way.'

With a grunt, the old man levered himself out of his sagging armchair and hurried to join her. In the dairy they found the calf stretched stiff on the concrete floor. Needles and syringes lay all around him while the vet, ghostly pale, rummaged in her bag, muttering to herself.

He was a decent-sized animal, eight months old. They were fattening him for their own freezer, an old-fashioned practice for a modern dairy farm, and Gemma found it a bit of a nuisance.

'I've never eaten shop-bought beef in my life and I don't intend to start now,' Alo always responded when she complained.

Today, the calf had been due for castration and to have his budding horns removed. Five minutes ago, Gemma had been leaning casually against the wall, watching the vet slide a carefully measured dose of sedative into the bulging vein, the first step in this minor, routine job.

'Calm down, woman!' Alo roared over the vet's babble. 'What are you doin' to get him back up on his feet?'

She had already given the animal adrenaline, twice as much as he should need.

'I haven't got a long enough needle to jab him straight into the heart.'

'Can you do nothin' more for him?'

Alo dragged the young vet bodily out of his way and hunkered down stiffly beside the prone calf. It was no longer breathing, the tear film already evaporating from the surfaces of its unblinking eyes. He reached into the old leather holster he wore on his belt and pulled out the ancient pen knife he used fifty times a day around the farm. His black thumbnail flicked out an attachment. It wasn't a blade, as far as Gemma could see, merely a long, sharp spike. She couldn't imagine what its purpose might be.

The old man grasped the beast's muzzle, as any stockman will do, and regarded it for just a moment. Then he spoke quietly but firmly into the young bull's ear.

'Get up outta that, ya lazy bastard.'

Abruptly, he rammed the length of the metal spike into the velvet-soft muzzle, splitting the septum right up to the hilt of the knife. The vet flinched and the last vestiges of colour left her lips and cheeks. Gemma readied herself to catch the young woman if she fell.

The bull's nostrils slammed open on the instant and he sucked in a huge, shuddering breath, rasping like a stone caught under a tight-fitting door.

'Good man yerself,' Alo exulted.

He grabbed a towel and started massaging the rough coat, rubbing warmth and life back into the spastic limbs. He glanced up at the vet.

'Acupuncture.'

'*What?*'

'Acupuncture point. Respiration centre.'

The women picked up the litter, matching every discarded needle to its case, until they were satisfied that no sharps remained to injure a valuable cow later on. Then Gemma declared she was taking the trembling vet to the house for tea.

'Put a good splash of brandy in it,' Alo ordered.

'Fuck sake, Alo. You can't give people brandy at eleven in the morning with the cops round every corner. *Sugar* is what she needs.'

Gemma half-led, half-pushed the vet into the warm farmhouse kitchen and wet the tea. Slowly a little colour returned to the woman's cheeks. Alo came in and sat opposite her.

'What in the name of God did you do to cause the calf to keel over like that?'

The young vet started her defence, her voice rising in pitch uncontrollably. She had done nothing wrong; she had given the right dose, the right drug. She had done nothing wrong. She didn't know what to do. She had done what she could. She had done nothing wrong.

Alo reached across the table, took her chin in his huge, calloused grip and turned her face gently towards his. The girl winced. She's afraid of him, Gemma thought, afraid of this crazy old man.

'So tell us what all you learned the day then, lassie?' Alo's voice was quiet.

She stared at him and didn't speak.

'I'll tell you, daughter dear. You've learned a clatter of important things the day. Firstly, sometimes things go wrong for no bloody reason at all. Secondly, everyone has something to teach, no matter how old and crazy they look.' He smiled self-deprecatingly before finishing his uncharacteristically long speech. 'And finally, you've learned that the most important thing in this life is to keep breathing. Breathing. You can call it *pranayama* if you want, but it's just breathing. That's the biggest difference of all between living and dying.'

He patted her hand and smiled. 'That business with the knife. That's a trick I saw used once over sixty years ago by Connors, the bonesetter. It was long before there was a vet within cycling distance of this yard. I reckon it must be acupuncture, though old man Connors wouldn't have known the word. I never hoped to have to do it myself.'

The vet looked down at the table. 'I didn't know what to do. I thought he was dying.'

'He *was* dying, pet, so what did I have to lose? Drink up your tea and give us your keys. I'll drive ye home.'

She salvaged enough dignity to drive herself home in the end, after a final look at her patient. The young bull was already staggering around drunkenly in a straw-bedded stall. The old man stayed to supervise its recovery while Gemma got on with the endless job of running a dairy farm.

Dusk fell over the yard. The evening milking had gone well, and for once there were no small outstanding jobs to do before the bedtime checks. Spuds were rattling and hissing on the hob, and Gemma and Alo sat in the kitchen waiting for Cormac to come home. He was doing a bit of overtime at the fabricator's shed where he now worked since handing over the running of the farm to his wife. The overtime salved his pride, for the absence of his half-hearted efforts on the land had scarcely been missed.

Gemma glanced over at her father-in-law. He hadn't mentioned the morning's events, nor would he. The episode was over for him. If she wished to discuss it, she would have to raise it herself.

'That was nice of you this morning,' she ventured. 'She thought you were going to eat her.'

Alo regarded her from under thick white eyebrows, composing his few words with care, as always. 'Aye, well, there's plenty around here who would have.'

He sighed quietly and placed his warm, rough hand over hers where it lay on the table between them. He frowned a little before speaking.

'Gemma, you know I never had a chance to have a girl-child, but I tell you this, if I'd had a daughter of my own, I'd make fine sure and rightly that no grumpy oul' farmer would make her cry over a scrawny Friesian bull not worth two hundred pounds.'

And that was all he was ever likely to say on the issue.

It was warm now in the kitchen. Last year Gemma had replaced, at vast expense, his old Electrolux cooker with an electric Aga. It ticked over day and night, heating the whole house and the water too. It was a marvel to Alo. His thoughts strayed to his wife Bid, stoking and cleaning their temperamental old coke-fired stove, coaxing fruit cakes and bread of extraordinary lightness out of it, muttering a persistent background of unheeded complaint.

'Why did I not buy her the bloody electric cooker she wanted?' he asked Gemma for the millionth time. '*God's sake woman, I used to say, do you think money grows on trees? Would we be cutting up the Farmers Journal and leaving yesterday's news inked on our backsides if I had the money for a brand new electric cooker?*'

Gemma patted his hand gently and glanced, as she had done so many times before, down the full length of the old pine table. It was a huge expanse of board – ten people could eat in comfort there. How long had it been since the big table was put to its proper use? She thought of Alo and the boy Cormac, sitting side by side, crammed together at one end, alone.

Bid was dead these forty years past. Ovarian cancer had ripped her from her home and her family in sixteen short, shocking weeks. Three decades later, hoping against almost extinct hope, Alo had noticed a pattern to Cormac's increased outings.

'I say, lad, is there e'er a sniff of a woman on the scene?'

Cormac had fobbed him off good-naturedly. 'Houl' yer whist, Da. D'you want me to bring home some young one who'll turf you out onto the road when she can't bear the slurry-smell any longer and we have to sell the farm to pay her divorce lawyer?'

Alo had waited and watched, praying that, in time, Cormac would bring him good news. His old friend Sean O'Neill had come downstairs one Sunday morning and found a half-naked young woman in his kitchen.

'She was wearing nothing but one of Junior's shirts,' Sean confided. 'Barely covered her ass. It was like a racing greyhound – just a few inches from the hair!'

The old men had roared at that while Sean Junior stood fit to kill them at the back door of the eleven o'clock Mass. He tried unsuccessfully to hush them, like a blushing old nun. Despite this unorthodox beginning, Junior and Helen had gone on to marry, and had produced two male children in four years.

Alo had longed for the day he might find a bare-limbed intruder in *his* kitchen. It never happened though. It would never have crossed Gemma's mind. He reckoned they hadn't had much of a sex life before their marriage. The house she'd shared with two other young women had been twenty minutes from the farm, a massive distance for a dairy farmer. Alo could count on the fingers of his work-roughened hands the number of times when Cormac had pulled into the farmyard in a cloud of smoke at seven in the morning, flustered, embarrassed and cursing. 'Quit yer gurnin now, Da, I'm warning you. I'm here now, amn't I?'

Perhaps that lack of sexual opportunity was part of the reason they had married so quickly. Alo's friends had nudged and winked. *Oh it'll be a fine baby, for sure. Ten pounds weight. Conceived on the honeymoon and born three months early.* Unfortunately not.

In years to come, after Alo's death, the big pine table would remain to bear witness to Cormac and Gemma holding hands alone together in the silence of the kitchen. Eventually, the heirless farm and the house would pass to someone who would replace the old table and fill the house with a big, noisy family. Gemma thought that the new owners might even see fit to pull the old house down. It was damp and dark and had had no major improvements for decades.

She looked over at the gruff, weather-beaten face of her father-in-law. Her heart swelled with sympathy and gratitude. He knew about love and loss. He was an old man, twenty years older than her own mother, but he was also a dairy farmer with a pedigree herd. He knew all about fertility when Gemma and Cormac were just starting out on that journey. She could look him in the eye and use words like 'cervix' and 'flush' and 'semen' and he didn't blush or look away. He knew that some pairings were destined to failure, and that sometimes neither prayer, nor medicine, nor surgery would change that fact.

Alo was no stranger to infertility. His Aunt Mae had been barren in the years when prayer was as much help to a woman as medicine, and he had told Gemma of Mae's efforts. Father Paul Deenan had helped to organise an expensive and lengthy pilgrimage to Lough Derg and to the Marian shrine faraway at Knock, in County Mayo. The journey through the civil war-torn country took a week by cart and bus, to no avail. An even more complicated illicit trip had taken place several years later to the Comeragh Mountains in Waterford. Mae had travelled the last leg of the exhausting journey, up the steep slopes of the mountain, on a small grey ass marked on his withers with the sign of the cross, a reminder that one of his race had been good enough for Our Lord and Saviour and was surely good enough for Mae O'Donovan. Guided by an ancient, well-paid tinker woman, devout, orthodox Mae had abjured her faith and hung a piece of rag on an ancient fairy tree, its magical powers revered by the gypsy women, and had sworn to bring a thanksgiving gift on her return trip the following year, after the promised confinement to come.

What complicated lie could have explained Mae's absence for such a long time to the curious ears of Father Deenan in the confessional, Gemma wondered. In the end poor Mae had not received her blessing, neither from the Christian nor the pagan source, and she had died an old woman, cared for by her nieces in a way that was probably a thing of the past.

Gemma looked out across the yard at the mobile home where she and Cormac still preferred to spend their nights. Its small windows blinked back at her accusingly.

'It's a temporary measure – just till the children outgrow the bedrooms,' Cormac had said. 'Then we'll build what we need.'

'Jesus, that won't take long,' Gemma snapped. 'Get a cot and a playpen and a high chair in here and we'll have to sleep on the roof.'

Over the long waiting-years, they had come to spend more and more time in the farmhouse with Alo. The old man's unconcealed love for his only son and his no-longer-young wife permeated every corner. Love disguised the peeling wallpaper. It illuminated the Sacred Heart and the Papal Blessing from Paul VI, bestowed on Alo's own short marriage. Love transfigured Gemma's dismal surroundings. It enfolded and cemented her marriage. It protected them all from the sudden pangs of grief that struck unbidden and without warning.

She took Alo's hand in hers and gently thumbed the ugly, purple warfarin blotches that poked out from under his frayed cuff. He covered her hand with his other one; a stack of hands, work-hardened and short-nailed. Two large hands. Two small ones. They sat united and waited for the man they loved.

Life could be a lot worse. They just had to keep on breathing.

A Real Woman

:::::

Everyone knows that Catholic priests are raving, slavering drunkards – even the teetotal ones – so you carefully set your tumbler down behind a large photograph of Pope Francis on the mantelpiece before you answer the front door of the parochial house. You take a moment to adjust the angle of the cheap gilt frame to hide your well-watered Powers. His Holiness doesn't seem to mind; his expression doesn't change. His benign smile says, *Never mind, my child. If I had to serve in that shithole parish of yours, I'd have a snifter myself the odd time.* Not a big man for the condemnations nor for letting fly the first stone, is Francis; more of a live-and-let-live fella, like yourself.

In earlier years you wouldn't have hidden the alcohol, not when Tomás Ó Fiaich was Primate of All Ireland – a jovial big lad out celebrating at the opening of every envelope in the diocese – and no one thought twice of a priest hopping in his car to administer the last rites with a few drops taken. Those days are gone though, and you pause with your hand on the door handle to crunch a Polo mint. You're not a big drinker and you've nothing to hide, but you're sick to the back teeth of snide remarks and snarky glances.

'Am I disturbing you, Father? I could come back later.'

A civil greeting anyway. That's good. You haven't a clue who the young lad is, and you don't bother trying to guess. You've always been hopeless with names. Back in the day you'd have started an old rigmarole of asking after his parents and hoping desperately for some chink of light to fall on the mystery of your visitor's name. There's no need for those subterfuges these days. Lads of this young man's vintage who darken the church door are as rare as hen's teeth, so much so that you personally know every one of them and all their seed and breed. Apart from funerals, this fella probably hasn't been in a church since the Passing Out Parade – or the Sacrament of Confirmation, as the school teachers still call it. *That doesn't mean he's a bad lad, of course.* Pope Francis smiles encouragingly.

'Come in, come in. Sure it's only eight o'clock. Let me turn off this noise.'

You cringe. Should elderly priests spend Saturday evenings watching *Strictly Come Dancing*? Who knows? Who cares these days? You're sure your visitor has never heard the phrase 'a vertical expression of a horizontal desire'; if his grandmother ever told him about Ireland's priests preaching from the pulpit about the sins of jazz and close-dancing, he'd probably think she was making it up. As your hand hovers over the remote, Jess and Brian on *Strictly* strut like feral ponies, all white teeth and tossing locks. You've been watching other people dance all your life. You're sure you could have given good account of yourself, if it wasn't for the bloody Roman collar and the lack of a partner.

'Will you take a cup of tea?' you ask.

Your visitor has sprawled, uninvited, across an easy chair, legs falling apart from the crotch, taking up a huge amount of space. Your space. You wouldn't want to share a bus seat with him.

That's another new thing for Irish people, this excessive taking up of space, this stating to the world, *Here I am. Take me or leave me.* Or more realistically, *Take me or fuck right off.*

'G'wan, g'wan, g'wan,' he replies and you smile patiently, as if he is the first person to make that joke. *Father Ted* has a lot to answer for.

'Mrs Doyle has the night off,' you say, your smile not reaching your eyes. 'Will I wet a pot of tea? To be honest, I haven't had a housekeeper for over ten years. I know where the kettle lives.'

'No, you're grand, Father, I'll not be here for long.'

Well thank God (if He exists) for small mercies.

'What can I do for you?' you ask, finally remembering that he is probably at the same disadvantage as yourself. You stick out your hand. 'I'm Father Anthony O'Donovan. Should be long since retired, but still holding the fort here in the absence of a younger man. Do me a favour and tell me you're here to discuss your vocation to the priesthood or diaconate. I could do with a hand.'

You laugh to show that you know you're being ridiculous. After a moment your visitor shrugs off his appalled look and tries to remember whatever manners he once knew.

'You're a real geg, Father. No such luck here. I'll have to work for my living, not join the priesthood.' He smiles to take the sting out of it, but you are long past caring about insults like these.

You glance at the clock sitting next to your hidden whiskey on the mantelpiece. The second half of *Strictly* is always where the competition comes down to the wire.

'Can you tell me why you're here, my child? Or do you need more time?'

Have you never heard of the Samaritans, you big lummox? They've a hape of specially trained listeners if all you want to do is not talk.

'God, no. Sorry. I'm right, now.'

He pauses and you fear he's going to lapse into silence again, but eventually a dark-red flush travels up from the open collar of his shirt and stains the whole of his stubbled face.

'Erm, it's confession, you see, Father. I'd like to go to confession.'

'Confession?'

You can't remember the last time a parishioner came to the parochial house looking for an out-of-hours confession. It used to be oul' dolls, rushing up with their semi-imaginary sins. Four terrifying times during the Troubles it had been shaking, pale-faced, bloodstained men vomiting out their awful deeds, pouring their pain into your heart and soul. You had known, even as you spoke the words of absolution, that you were partaking in a charade, that despite their honest repentance they were doomed now, doomed to repeat their crimes when ordered, or die for refusing to do so.

You take a careful look at your penitent's face, in case you need to describe him to the cops later, and check his boots and clothes, but they are clean. He just looks … ordinary. He isn't wearing a Victorian waistcoat or sporting a bun in his hair or the beard of an Old Testament patriarch. Nor has he shaved his head and covered every inch of visible skin with swirling, interlinked Celtic tattoos. He just looks normal. He looks like a lad who might be on the second string football team at Clann na nGael GAA club.

'You know, the Sacrament of Reconciliation is available on Friday evenings, before the devotions –' you begin.

'Tonight, Father, it has to be tonight.'

You sigh.

'And then I need you to write me a letter confirming that I done it.'

'What?'

'I need a letter confirming that I done my confession tonight, otherwise I won't get my papers and the girlfriend will have my guts.'

'What papers? What are you talking about? Your girlfriend …?'

He drags himself into an approximation of a respectful posture.

'I'm sorry, Father, I'll start at the start. The girlfriend and me is getting married. She's hankering for a baby. Nothin'll do her but up the aisle and straight into the maternity ward nine months later.'

'Have you given this some serious thought? That's a big step.'

'Ach, we're together eight years. She's had her days drinking Prosecco through a straw and dancing on the table. Now she wants the ring and the baby.'

'And she wants them in that order? How unusual.'

You didn't mean to say that out loud, but it's water off a duck's back to him.

'Look, it's simple. We've one day over us on the pre-marriage course and the final day's tomorrow and I need to do the confession and get the proof that it's done.'

'Why here? Why now? Surely the Sacrament of Reconciliation was offered you today as part of the preliminary proceedings?'

You wish the Vatican would stop messing with the names of everything, chopping and changing for the sake of it, it seemed. The old grey cells in the old grey heads of your congregation can't keep up with all these subtle changes in the creeds and responses. It's like the Tower of Babel at Mass these days, with half of them on the Vatican II responses and half on the new ones. At least *Sacrament of Reconciliation* has a chance of catching on. Who the hell came up with the *sacrament of penance* version? No one in the twenty-first century thinks they deserve penance.

151

The man shifts uneasily in his chair. 'There's no way on God's earth I'm doing my confession and then having Laura going straight in after me to the same priest. He'd be looking at her and thinking, *what the fuck are you doing with that gobshite, wee girl?'*

He doesn't apologise for swearing in front of you, or even seem to be aware of how inappropriate it is.

'Well, surely the priest in charge should have reassured you on that front,' you say. 'The secrets of the confessional are sacred unto the grave. He'd never have said anything to her. Nor would he have wanted to. The confessor is merely a channel between the repentant penitent and the eternal, boundless mercy of God, not a judge, jury or executioner.'

'Yeah, right.'

'My child – ' And suddenly curiosity gets the better of you, and you can't keep up the pretence any longer. 'Listen, son, you want me to hear your confession? Just give me two ticks.'

You bustle back a few minutes later, robed and ready, more than half expecting to find him gone, along with the silver candlesticks (which aren't actually silver) and your wallet, which you stupidly left in the pocket of your jacket hanging on the back of a chair. But he is lolling in the armchair, waiting.

You sit down beside him and wait for him to start. He looks at you blankly.

'Bless me, Father, for I have sinned ...' you say by way of a prompt, but he doesn't know the next part. 'How long is it since your last confession?' you ask.

'Oh right, yeah. It might be ten years ... no, wait ... it must be sixteen or seventeen years ago. First year in the college, I'd guess.'

'When you were about eleven years old?'

'I'd say so.'

'And never since?'

'Never felt the need, to be honest.'

'Because you have a personal relationship with God and feel you don't need the mediator of a priest?'

'What? Shit, no. Look, I just don't think I ever done anything you could call a sin.'

'Well, that's great.' You pause to digest that piece of information. 'If that's the case why didn't you go to confession this morning and tell that to the priest who took the course – Father Manus was it?'

'Big, round beardy fella? A bird's nest poking out of each nostril?'

You snort, but change it into a cough. 'That's the one. Why didn't you just tell him you'd nothing on your conscience? Or make something up?'

'Lie to a priest? Lie in the confession box?'

You're surprised at the tone of shock, as if you had offered to stab his mother or lend him a JCB to gouge the cash machine out of the wall of the Ulster Bank.

'Well, I'm here now, my child. I don't know how you found me, or what brings you out here to the side of this windy hill when there's priests a lot closer to Omagh than I am, but let's do it. Do you know the Act of Contrition?'

He shakes his head, so you guide him through the children's version and he repeats it line for line. You can see signs of recognition in his eyes as bits come back to him, and he looks quite pleased with himself when he blurts out the final words without prompting. Then silence.

'I didn't love God when ...' you hint.

He squints at you as though you've sprouted satanic horns while he searches for the words; then realisation dawns.

'I didn't love God when ...' He stops. 'I feel a bit thick doing this.'

153

You nod and smile. The dancers have finished; you'll have to watch *Strictly* online tomorrow. Maybe, just maybe, you might be able to help this young man and Laura start married life unencumbered, shrived and psychologically sound. It would feel good to matter, to know that you still can justify your existence.

'Listen, Father, there's no point beating around the bush.' He rubs his hands across his eyes like a much older man and drops his gaze. 'It's a sex thing. I wouldn't necessarily have been completely faithful over the years, like.'

'Well, eight years is a long time, I suppose, and you would have been very young …'

'Well yes, there's that, I suppose.'

'So you want to clear your conscience of the weight of having betrayed your fiancée. And the other girl, of course – I mean, it wasn't fair on her either.'

'Well, I want the absolution. And I want the letter.'

'Yes, I can see how you wouldn't want to start a marriage with this hanging over you.'

'That's right.'

'So, you're sorry for your youthful indiscretions, and you resolve never to sin in this way again and remain faithful. That's the right frame of mind for any young man embarking on matrimony.'

He should jump on that. You practically patted his shoulder and told him he's a great fella. He should be looking you in the eye by now and declaring before God that he's feeling a million dollars, and that it won't be another seventeen years before he comes back to confession. But he isn't.

You follow the line of his stare. His eyes are fixed on the toes of your shoes, cheap and not particularly comfortable, but shiny and black and recently polished.

'When was the last time you saw this other girl?' you ask, your heart sinking like the lead-weighted eel-fishing nets of Lough Neagh.

'Last week.'

'Last week? For fuck's sake!' That gets his attention all right. He jumps and shifts in his seat. 'I'm sorry. You gave me a shock … Last week? And do you love this girl?'

'Of course I love her. Sure we're getting married in six weeks.'

'The other one, you big amadán. Do you love this other girl?'

He laughs. Whatever you were expecting – self-recrimination, shame, even claims that he was led astray – you weren't expecting laughter.

'Of course not. Catch yourself on. Sure she's not even a real woman.'

And now you are truly out of your depth. You've heard some crazy stuff over the years, but what are you going to say to this man?

'A doll, you mean? Is it one of those inflatable sex dolls?'

Please, please God, let it be a doll. Don't let it be some kind of robot. Do such things exist yet? *Oh Christ, don't let it be … a child.*

· 'No, Father. Jesus, no!' He looks at you in horror. 'I'm not some kind of pervy freak. It's you know …' He nods and winks.

'I certainly do not.'

'It's a business relationship.'

'You work with her?'

'For Christ's sake, do I have to spell it out? They're working girls. Prossies.'

You sink back in your seat. 'They? They? You're seeing prostitutes and you're getting married in six weeks?'

You rest your forehead in the palm of your hand and stare at the worn carpet. Horrified by your pragmatism, you ask, 'What if you catch something? What if you give a disease to your wife? Or the unborn child?'

'Ah now, Father, do you think I'm as thick as a plate of champ? There's such a thing as condoms you know. And the girls look after themselves. I mean, they're not street-walkers.'

You hold up your hand; you honestly don't want to know any more. 'Listen. I'm heading for seventy-five years old. I don't want to talk about what you do to these poor misfortunate women.'

'Ach, they're grand, Father. The minders look after them okay.' He glances down and you watch him twist his fingers together. 'Well, there was one girl last month wouldn't stop crying ... but usually they're grand.'

You look up at Francis for help. Christ, you need that whiskey now, and another stronger one to wash it down.

'Are you telling me you had intercourse with a prostitute who was crying?' When it's obvious he's not going to answer, you continue. 'Why didn't you stop? Why didn't you do something? You could have called the police.'

'She told me not to stop. She said she was sorry, that she'd be okay the next time, to keep going and not give her a bad review.'

'Next time?'

'Well, I think that's what she said. She was a wee foreign girl with a thick enough accent.'

You stagger to your feet and pull the stole off from round your neck. Its weight is bearing you to the ground. In your trouser pocket is a cheap, tinny rosary ring. You have got in the habit of carrying these rings around with you because the children and grandchildren of your parishioners are so divorced from the Church that you sometimes turn up at a wake to discover that the corpse has no rosary entwined between its fingers. You pull out the ring and slip it on your finger, just for the superstitious comfort it gives you, and lean heavily against the mantelpiece.

The world has gone mad, the whole boiling lot of them, and this lad's the worst. Your searching fingers close around the hidden cut-glass tumbler and you drink the whole lot in two gulps. It is more than half water anyway.

'I don't know what you want or why you came here,' you say, 'but it's time to go.'

'You're behind the times, Father. It's just a job. There's nothing to be ashamed of, like. It's just a service industry like any other.'

'They've nothing to be ashamed of – you're probably right. But you?' Your voice shakes and you turn to the sideboard to claim the Powers; no water this time as the bottle rattles a shaky staccato on the rim of the glass. 'What the hell is wrong with you? You've a woman wants to marry you and you're messing around with prostitutes. Isn't one woman enough for you?'

He laughs and you clench the full lead Tyrone Crystal glass so hard you think it might shatter in your hand, but it has been tempered at thousands of degrees Celsius and it withstands the puny heat of your fury.

'For Christ's sake, it's not the same thing at all,' he says, pausing for a moment to clarify in his own mind exactly why it's not the same thing at all. 'I mean, you wouldn't do that kind of stuff to a real woman.'

The heavy tumbler catches him on the cheekbone. Thank God there's no bleeding. If you still had a housekeeper it would be hard to explain the whiskey splashes on the heavily patterned wallpaper. There's even a splash on the face of the Sacred Heart, which catches the light of the red votive lamp below and glows eerily, as though Our Lord is crying blood.

He touches the side of his face, which is reddening now, and you find yourself wondering if anyone saw him arrive here. If they come tomorrow morning and find you lying in a pool of your own blood, with the Sacred Heart on one wall and his Blessed Mother on the other staring impassively down, would they be able to trace him and arrest him? Maybe that would be the best way to save Laura from this marriage. Or maybe you should ring young Father Manus and say, *fuck the seal of the confessional, wait till you hear this*.

His fingers stop probing his face. It doesn't look too bad to you; his eye isn't swelling. He'll probably just have a big, easily explained-away bruise. He could say he walked into a door. Isn't that what the women of your parishes have been saying to you for the last forty years? You used to marvel at how clumsy women were.

He steps towards you and you cringe backwards, wish to hell the door was closer, or your mobile phone. He reaches out a hand and lifts his car keys from where you didn't notice he had thrown them and turns to leave.

'I take it I'm not getting my letter then,' he says. 'I'll take your advice and go to confession tomorrow. Tell bushy-nose a pack of lies. Hypocrisy. I can't stand hypocrisy. But look where the truth gets you.'

You watch as he leaves the room, not even slamming the door, and listen to him quietly driving off into the night. You turn to the mantelpiece, gripping it with white knuckles, and lay your head on the cooling slab of marble.

Pope Francis says to you, clear as day, 'Fuck's sake, Antonio, get yourself another glass and fill it. And have one for me.'

Love in the Age of Internet Banking

:::::

Sonia stands at the cashier's desk and clutches the edge tightly to stop herself from collapsing onto the floor.

'But there must be a mistake. I had five grand, give or take, in there last month.'

'I'm really sorry, but the balance is three hundred, and that's including the child benefit that only came in half an hour ago.'

'But ... but ... I've direct debits going out tomorrow – mortgage, life insurance.'

'I'm really sorry. It looks like you've been hacked. I'll call my manager.'

Sonia feels the blood drain from her cheeks and a pounding in her chest. 'What am I going to do? I had to leave the week's messages sitting in a trolley in Dunnes to come round here. I told them I'd be back to pay for them after I got this sorted out.'

'Don't worry, love,' the cashier says, 'it happens more often than you'd think. There's insurance to cover it. It'll get sorted out. The hackers win some, and they lose some. Sometimes we can even trace exactly what house they're sitting in when they do the transactions.'

'And will they go to jail?'

'Ah God, no. Most of them are abroad, even the Irish ones. They wouldn't be thick enough to rob bank accounts in their own countries.'

The manager's office is tiny, windowless, with paperwork spilling out of big manila folders on the desk and floor and on top of the filing cabinets that line the walls. Sonia had imagined a broad expanse of oak desk and a PA carrying in cups of freshly brewed coffee, but the manager tells her she's been watching too much TV.

Click. Click. Tap, tap, tap. The manager swipes the mouse angrily, then gives the roller ball a brisk rub on the sleeve of her cardigan and tries again.

Double click. Name, address, telephone number.

'This is weird. This looks bad …'

'What? What? What could be worse than losing five grand?'

'I'm really sorry, Mrs Farrell, but give me a moment to work out what's going on here.'

'You can call me Sonia.'

The other woman nods and returns to her clicking, screen after screen appearing on the monitor that Sonia can just glimpse out of the corner of her eye without straining too obviously. Giving up the squinting as a bad job, she has a good look around the small room.

In pride of place, on the only filing cabinet without a teetering stack of folders, sits a bedraggled peace lily and a framed photo of a happy, smiling family: the manager herself beaming a huge mouthful of expensive dentistry, with a squat, heavy man, two beautiful boys and, in the background, the unmistakable spires of a Disney castle.

'Are those your boys? Did you go to Paris, or Orlando?'

The manager looks up briefly from her frenzied clicking and smiles. 'Paris. Last year. Bloody freezing, and it rained three days out of the five. But it was good, like.'

'I wanted to take my kids to Disney.' And, without warning, the tears spill down onto the cheap veneer of the manager's desk. 'Ignore me, I'm just being stupid. I'm a mess at the moment. I'm splitting up with my husband.'

'Oh Jesus!'

'What? What?'

The manager has stopped her frantic clicking and searching and is now looking down at the keyboard in silence.

'You should have told me you were separating.'

'Why? What difference does it make?' Sonia's voice wobbles and she gives a little cough to steady it. 'I haven't even told my own mother yet. She's going to have a fit. Thinks I'm a spoilt, lazy stay-at-home mother and that the sun shines out of Donal's hole. *That man clean ruins you*, she says. She says I'm *one lucky bitch* and haven't even the sense to know it.' Sonia laughs and stares down at her left ring finger where the indentation from the absent wedding ring is still clearly visible. 'God, I'm really sorry. That was totally inappropriate.'

'Your husband's a real charmer is he?'

'Oh, he'd charm the birds out of the trees, talk them into the oven, and they'd thank him for it. He's fucking gorgeous too, and my mother's a fool for a good-looking man.'

The manager pushes her chair back a little on its wheels and swivels round so that she and Sonia are face-to-face, eye to eye. 'Is your husband good at computers?'

'Yeah, he's brilliant.'

'And who set up your online banking?'

'I don't know. It was years ago.'

And then the penny finally drops.

Sonia covers her face with her hands and moans. The manager goes over to the Ballygowan water dispenser and comes back with a plastic cup full of water, but it's too cold and Sonia winces as it hits her fillings. The flimsy cup would have buckled in her hand, spilling the water down her front, if the manager hadn't gently taken it from her.

'The new iPad, a couple of months ago. He said he would set it up. He said I wouldn't use the memory to its full advantage. He said it would just end up being an expensive toy, so better to let him set it up instead.'

'Jesus, it's not in your handbag is it?'

'No, why? It's at home.'

'What kind of phone do you have?'

'It's an iPhone 5. It's Donal's old one.'

'Turn it off.'

'Are you fucking serious? It's not like he's spying on me from the office in Belfast. Catch a grip of yourself.'

'Turn it off.'

Sonia scrabbles around in her handbag and turns the phone off. The first clammy hands of dread start to close around her heart.

'Mrs Farr ... Sonia.' The manager wipes her hands on her skirt and starts again. 'Sonia, people's internet banking gets hacked all the time – a careless transaction on a dodgy website, one of the kids in the App Store buying Minecraft add-ons behind your back, even a card skimmer at the ATM. These things happen. It's cheaper for the insurance and the bank to refund victims than to pay enough tellers to sit in the branches nine to five, Monday to Friday, doling out tens and fifties. So we force people online, even my old grandad who wouldn't know cyber security from the back of his arse.'

'Like me, you mean?'

'Yes, Sonia, like you.' She sighs and takes a minute to compose her thoughts before looking Sonia in the eye. 'Did you and your husband decide to separate last Thursday?'

'You make it sound so civilised. I told him to fuck off out of my life, once and for all.'

'Everything's gone, Sonia. I'm so very, very sorry.'

'The whole five grand? Oh my God.'

'No. Not five grand. Everything. Hackers hack one compromised account, take what they can and move on. But this is different. Someone has been systematically emptying your accounts since last Thursday. Every day. Every account, the maximum daily limit. Your savings account, the joint account, the mortgage account – the only thing you have left is four and a half grand in a seven-day notice account.'

'I hate that bloody account. It's such a pain in the hole. That's why I stopped making deposits into it.'

'Well, it's the only one you have left, and there's two days left on the notice that was given on Thursday. I'll cancel that now.' She types and taps and clicks before standing up again and collecting a freshly printed page and giving Sonia a copy.

'Well, look on the bright side – at least the insurance company will know who he is,' Sonia says. 'Oh Christ, if they press charges my ma will have an absolute seizure. It'll be in the papers and all over the place I suppose.'

The manager goes back to her own side of the table and sits down heavily, a defeated puff of breath popping out as she lands on the poorly upholstered chair.

'I'm afraid it's *game over, thanks for playing*, Sonia. You haven't a leg to stand on. You gave him access to your accounts. You failed to keep your passwords secret. You broke every rule of cyber-banking. Can you tell me your husband's password and registration number?'

'No.' It is a whisper, a broken, fragile sound.

'No. Can you tell me approximately how many bank accounts he owns?'

'No.'

'Do you know how much money he has, even a rough guess?'

'Yes, that much I do know. He has either a hundred grand or fuck all. Every penny he's earned for the last three years – or longer for all I know – has gone to Paddy Power.' Sonia smiles through the tears which are running unheeded through her foundation. 'That's what the break-up is about. I can't keep living like this. It was bad enough when I used to walk past the bookie's door and wonder if he was in there, licking up to that big fat frump Sarah Brady, but now he doesn't even have to leave the house. American baseball, Chinese soccer leagues, Brexit, Trump, two flies walking up the wall. Tapping away on the laptop, buying me even more fucking jewellery when he wins and not having the mortgage money when he loses. Two cars in the driveway, a thousand pounds-worth of flat screen TV to watch the fucking racing on, and some mornings I don't know whether we can afford cornflakes for the kids' breakfast.'

Sonia stops and heaves a shuddering breath into her lungs.

'You're the first person I've told. I actually feel a bit better. I'm really sorry for vomiting that all out on top of you at work.'

'Every month, Sonia' – the manager sighs – 'every single month we have a woman in here telling me some version of the same story.'

'And men, too, of course,' Sonia says. 'I mean it's not like there aren't plenty of women out there fucking up their families' lives?'

'I've never once in ten years met a woman who knew all her husband's password. I don't know Jason's.' She glances over at the photograph. 'He sure as hell will never know mine.'

::::::

Sonia goes home with four thousand, eight hundred pounds between her and penury, and a list of new bank accounts. She needs a new laptop or iPad and a new phone, although she can't yet bring herself to believe what she has been told about tracking devices, listening apps and spyware. She needs a mortgage holiday. She needs to start thinking if she can live without a car; can the children walk to the activities for which she can no longer afford to pay? She needs to find out which sofa that bastard is sleeping on and go over and lamp the head off him and scream and rake her nails down his face.

But first she needs to ring Dunnes Stores and tell them she'll not be back for the laden trolley, that she is on her way to Lidl instead, with fifty-nine pounds in her purse and empty slots in her wallet where her bank cards used to be.

And the manager has told her to go to Father O'Donovan, the treasurer of St Vincent de Paul, and tell him that she's going to need to claw back some of the hundreds – or thousands – of pounds she has dropped into the charity box every Sunday at Mass, when she and Donal and the kids – hair shining, perfect make-up, dressed to the nines – paraded up to the front pews of St Cecilia's, half a mile from the derelict shell of the hall where she got her nickname all those years ago.

Sonia's luck has run out at last.

A Fine Big Buck

:::::

The ball soared through the air on a wave of whistling and screaming, whacked off the upright and flew straight back into the arms of the opposing right half forward. He booted it back to the forty-five metre line.

'Fuck sake,' said Alo, spitting pensively onto the ground. 'Take yer points, McCreish, and the goals will come.'

'Barry McCreish was always a bloody glory-hunter,' agreed Sean O'Neill.

McCreish, the Drumaleish full forward, charged back into the fray, red-faced and panting, huge circles of sweat clearly visible in the armpits of his green and gold top, pretending to be deaf to the mutters of complaint from the sideline.

'He's a heavy big lad, all the same, is McCreish. No stranger to the knife and fork.'

'Jesus Christ, Alo, that's putting it mildly. He's well past slaughter weight. He'll give himself a coronary if he's not careful.

Then Ballydowney will win for sure. Five fuckin' years in a row.'

'I'll tell you what, them selectors couldn't pick their own nose.'

'It's not like they've all the players in the world to pick from, I suppose.' Sean sighed and glanced around. 'Where are they all, Alo? The O'Connors and the McGlones and the Devlins? When we were lads, every fella in the parish was at training twice a week.'

'Sure, what the hell else was there to do in those days?'

'Now they're all sitting on their holes playing their wee computer games.'

'Or in Australia, drinkin' and whorin',' said Iggy Conlon, who had a son in Brisbane and another in Melbourne, only two children gone foreign out of seven, which was nothing much to complain of these days.

'Lucky bastards.'

A commotion broke out on the half-way line. Ciaran Hughes had a fistful of Michael Connolly's shirt and their two faces were locked together, snarling and spitting venom.

'Jesus, look at them two latchikos. Best friends since Primary One, shared every damn thing in their lives except parish and club, and still can't keep their fists off each other on the field.'

The referee took down both names and flashed two yellow cards.

'Hardly seems fair. Thon ref should a gone to Specsavers,' Iggy moaned.

'Up yer hole, referee!' shouted Sean. 'A fuckin' yella; for having the shirt near tore off yer back!' He sighed. 'Connolly should complain about that.'

'Ah, look, I dare say he deserved it,' said Alo. 'Connolly's always talking when he should be listening. Fuck knows what he said to Hughes.'

'Pity Hughes doesn't live three miles closer to town in Drumaleish parish. He'd be a man to have on yer team alright. Even so, the ref's a wanker.'

'Would yis catch a grip of yerselves, for the love of God. A fine example you're setting to the kids. Look at yis – three oul' eejits guldering at the referee. You'd think it was the All-Ireland final.' Alo's daughter-in-law, Gemma, had had enough. 'How many All-Ireland medals do you have yourself, Sean?'

'Ah, piss off,' he said laughing.

'Gemma, love,' said Alo, 'leave us a little bit of joy in our lives. What have Sean and Iggy and I got left except the long, slow descent into the grave and a few pennies in our pockets for a pint after the match?'

'Jesus, speak for yourself. I've another twenty years in me and I'm beating off the women with a stick every week after bingo. As for you, you're rich as creosote and twice as sticky.'

Gemma tried to steer the conversation. 'Is your Malachy playing in the minors now, Sean?'

'Yip, that's right, our Junior's oldest boy. He's supposed to be doing his A levels but he doesn't give a flying fiddler's fuck about anything except making the Tyrone football team and looking in the mirror. He was for trying to grow one a them fuckin' bird's-nest beards, but the girlfriend gave him a can of Gillette foam at his eighteenth birthday party above in the hall. Do you mind that, Alo?'

'I do. I thought I was going to burst my hole laughing at him ripping off the wrapper and the whole parish and club knowing what it was afore he did.'

A roar went up from the opposite end of the pitch – three Ballydowney men closing in on the barely defended goal. A hand pass, a solo, a quick jouk to the right, then the ball barrelling straight and true towards the Drumaleish net. At the last possible second, the keeper got the very tips of his fingers to it, sending it in a slow arc out to be captured by his left half back and booted up towards Alo and the gang to safety.

Whoops and cheers and catcalls.

'Thon keeper's not the worst,' admitted Alo grudgingly.

'We're lucky to have him,' said Sean, 'wherever the fuck we found him.'

'Give it a rest, Sean,' snapped Gemma. 'You know fine rightly he was born in Craigavon hospital and has been living here on Market Street this ten years or more.'

'A fine big buck he is too. Grand long arms on him,' said her father-in-law.

'Jesus Christ, Alo,' hissed Gemma. 'I won't tell you again. You can't say that.'

'And I'm telling you again, Gemma love, I've been calling half the lads on that team *fine big bucks* since they were playing in the Under Thirteens, and every team afore them since about nineteen and fifty. I'm not going to change my way of speaking now. I wouldn't remember, even if I wanted to.'

'Relax, Gemma,' said Sean. 'It's not like he called him a nig-nog or anything. Although that's what we'd all have called him not so long ago, yourself included.'

'It's different. It's different now. We didn't know any better then.' Gemma winced and glanced over at Iggy Conlon, who seemed remarkably unperturbed by the conversation. 'You don't say things like that any more, Alo. You wouldn't call Bobby Willis over there an Orange bastard, would you? Not in this day and age.'

'Course I would, love, and I'll bet my bottom dollar he calls us Fenians and taigs when he's talking to his own. Although fair play to Willis – first Orangie ever was on the Drumaleish GAA team, nor ever came through the gates of the place, whatever crazy cross-community notion took hold of him all them years ago.'

'Well, you can't call Caleb a *buck*, whatever the hell else you want to call him, not when you can Google the word *slavery* and see the bills of sale offering *bucks* and *fertile women* – and kids – for a fiver. Iggy, will you for God's sake talk some sense into these two dinosaurs.'

'My own granddaughter is as black as the ace of spades,' said Iggy. 'I'll call young Obi Wan Kenobe whatever the fuck I want.'

'Obenkawa,' said Alo.

'You can't just make exceptions for the people you care about, Iggy,' said Gemma. 'That's like saying *some of my best friends are Protestant, but …*'

Iggy laughed. 'Some chance.'

'How is young Saoirse?' asked Alo. 'She settled in the very best and never a bother on her, isn't that right?'

Gemma looked down at the grass and cursed silently. Now she would have to listen to Iggy give them a blow-by-blow account of his granddaughter, adopted from Vietnam, and silently absorb the unspoken reproaches, the quiet air of bafflement that she and Cormac had never swooped out to some foreign land and returned with the heir to Alo's farm – her farm now – be he white, black or polka-dotted.

The keeper sprang in the air, his hands stretching, straining, reaching nine, nine-and-a-half feet off the ground, then gathered the ball tightly to his chest and hoofed it back into play.

'A fine, strong big … fella … right enough,' said Alo. 'I told you, look at the span of his arms.'

'As long as King Kong's,' said Sean.

Gemma stormed back to the car, shaking her head, and slammed the door.

'Women!' said Sean. 'Jesus, you can't please them.'

'You don't try very hard though, do you, Sean?' said Alo. 'Do you remember when the first batch of incomers arrived, working at the pig factory – big brown lads from Brazil and what have you?' His friends nodded. 'D'you mind how strange it seemed? You'd be standing in the queue for a bit of ice cream after Mass on a Sunday and they'd be gabbling away.'

'What's yer point?' asked Sean.

'I'm getting there. Do you mind the first day we saw a big crowd of childer piling out the door of the Sacred Heart College, and here and there a brown face, or a black one, and how strange it was? And then, a few years later, I saw a girl coming outta the girls' school with her wee scarf around her face and covering up her hair.'

'I hate that. Bloody disgraceful it is,' said Sean.

'D'you know what it puts me in mind of?'

'What, Alo?'

'It puts me in mind of my mother and my aunties and every second woman in this town back when I was young. Every one of them wore a headscarf whether it was raining or not, and no one ever looked twice at them. Fancy black lace mantillas for Mass too.'

'That's totally different, Alo, and you know it.'

'How, Sean? How's it different? How is forcing a woman out of the headscarf she wants to wear one bit kinder than forcing her into one she doesn't? Mebbe we should all just mind our own business.'

A point sailed over the bar at the Ballydowney end, McCreish making up for past sins, and the three old men nodded and smiled but didn't clap or cheer for fear McCreish would get too up himself.

Iggy looked around and dug the toe of his boot into the wet grass of the sideline and coughed. A pronouncement was coming, a rare thing from Conlon.

'The first few years when I used to see the kids walking down the footpath towards me in town, black and white and yella and headscarfs and whatever you're having yourself, I used to think to myself, *that's good, that's good. Our wee Saoirse'll have an easier time of it if the people gets used to all them incomers – she'll not stand out so much.*'

The men nodded and waited while Iggy marshalled his thoughts.

'Now when a big gaggle of them kids is walking towards me, d'you know what I think?'

'What's that, then?'

'I think, *fuckin' kids, taking up the whole footpath. No respect to make way for an oul' fella like me. Have they no homes to go to?* And after they're gone past I couldn't tell you, if my life depended on it, who they were or what they looked like, what language they were talking. Nor do I care.'

'And that's good is it?'

'Yes, Sean, that's good,' said Iggy. 'I mind well when I was a child coming out the school gate. You'd take yer tie off and you'd hide your school geansaí in yer bag for fear you'd meet a big gang of Prods on yer way home. And you'd look at the face of every approaching stranger and you'd wonder if today was going to be the day. And you'd say to yerself, *don't be bloody stupid, Iggy Conlon. Don't you know that most Prods aren't like that, the exact same way most of yer own friends aren't like that. Mostly we all just want to get home safe and fast.*'

The men nodded.

'But in the back of yer head there'd be this wee voice saying, *but mebbe this Prod's the one. It only takes one. Mebbe today is the day –* and you'd walk that wee bit faster. And for all you know, he was thinking the exact same thing about you.'

He looked up, and to the horror of his audience there was a hint of dampness at the corner of each eye. 'Well, our wee Saoirse can't take off her skin and hide it in her school bag, and that's why I say, yes, it's a good thing.'

'You know,' said Alo, 'when we were childer, every man jack in the country was as white as a sheet and we spent our whole lives dividing ourselves into Orange and Black and Green. Haven't we a fair cheek to look over at Obenkawa there and call him coloured?'

'Jesus Christ, listen to Martin Luther fuckin' King.' Sean O'Neill shook his head in disgust.

The referee blew the final whistle.

Drumaleish 2–12; Ballydowney 0–15.

Conversations Gemma Doesn't Want to Have Any More . . .

:::::

They are so expensive . . .

'I love your boots, Lucy. How the hell do you stand up for a whole day in them? They must be five inches high.'

'Ah thanks, Gemma. God, isn't it a terror to be in the winter boots already in the first week of September?'

'Well, you know me – I'm in my boots every day.'

'I'll do you a quick search on eBay and find you a pair of sparkly wellies with four-inch heels.'

Lucy's online shopping kept the small local post office going, with dozens of returns each week. Agnes Johnston, the post mistress, called Lucy her best friend.

'I'd look well in them, right enough,' said Gemma. 'Think I'll stick with the fleece-lined Dunlops from the co-op.'

'Ah, you're a real sex-kitten in your wellies – like my granny with the fluffy lining poking outta her slippers.'

'Piss off.' Gemma stretched down and felt the supple, butter-soft leather of her sister-in-law's boots. 'Gorgeous. I'd say I'd get a lifetime's supply of Dunlops for what you paid for those ones.'

'These are ancient. I bought them in BT's on Grafton Street when Jim and I went down to Dublin for our third wedding anniversary, and that's not today nor yesterday.'

'They're probably Prada or something, knowing you.' Gemma was just curious, not envious. She could afford any boots she wanted.

Lucy laughed and nodded. 'They cost a fucking fortune, but I look after them. New heels and soles every year. I wouldn't be able to replace them, no way. I used to have money. Now I have children.'

The silence stretched just a moment too long.

'Shit. Sorry, Gemma. That came out wrong.'

They are such a bloody nuisance …

'Cheers, ladies! Here's to 1991 – big hair, blue eyeshadow and Whitney Houston.'

'Speak for yerself, Cathy,' said Noeleen. 'I'll have you know that by 1991 I was wearing black from head to toe, ninety per cent of it out of the oul' man's section in War on Want, listening to The Jesus and Mary Chain and stamping around in sixteen-hole Doc Martens. My ma was down on her knees saying novenas that I'd be normal again before our Caroline's confirmation photos.'

The six women laughed and clinked glasses of Prosecco.

'To 1991.'

'To us.'

'Twenty-five years! Fuck!'

'Here's to War on Want and the Army Surplus store!'

At other tables the banter was rising high as the class of '91 mingled and chatted, accompanied by the odd cry of delight or the occasional embarrassed silence when a name or a face escaped them. Here and there a bored, vaguely intimidated man sucked morosely at a pint of Guinness.

'Who the fuck would bring their husband to this shindig?' said Gemma, laughing. 'Imagine Cormac stuck in the middle of this!'

'Or their wife,' said Cathy, looking down at her left hand where a solid gold band glinted dully in the subdued lighting. 'Anita asked if she should come, but I told her she'd be bored out of her mind. She'd spend the whole night being asked who she was and what class she was in and people apologising to her for not remembering her.'

'How'd she take that?'

'Ach, she saw the sense in it eventually. I mean, no one's gonna look over at that fella and wonder if was he in class S4B but decided to have a quick sex-change operation.' They all glanced over at the man, abandoned by his wife, who was surreptitiously watching a football match on his phone. 'I just didn't want to put Anita in a position where she had to explain herself all fucking night to a bunch of people she'll never see again.'

'Until 2041,' said Noeleen.

'Christ, we'll all be pushing seventy in 2041,' said Cathy.

'If we're lucky,' said Gemma. 'The alternative is worse.'

They all nodded.

'Poor Sarah Brady,' said Cathy. 'Jesus, when I heard she'd died I had to think a moment to remember the name.'

'I'd say she never recovered from her rough start in life,' said Sonia. 'It can't have been much fun in the Good Faith House.'

'Well, at least she had us,' said Noeleen with a smile. 'At least for a few years in primary school she had good friends and could have a bit of fun with us. I always liked Sarah. If she'd come on here to the Loreto with us we'd have looked after her.'

The other women glanced down at the table, uncertain whether to challenge Noeleen, until Sonia raised her glass with a forced smile.

'At least in 2041 we won't have to be watching what we drink and going home early so as not to upset the fucking babysitter.'

Sonia's chin quivered and Cathy leaned over and rubbed her arm. Sonia's life had gone to hell since she'd kicked out her waste-of-space-husband and he'd taken all their money. Gemma stretched across the table to the ice bucket and tipped the dregs of the bottle of bubbly into Sonia's glass.

'Yeah, the kids can come and collect us instead,' Noeleen said.

'About time they did something fucking useful for a change. All mine ever do is eat. Every time I open my kitchen door there's a child's arse sticking out of my fridge.'

'Don't talk to me. Fucking parasites.'

'And the smell! Oh my God, Sonia, just wait a few years until yours hit their teens. The air in my boys' bedroom would kill a canary,' said Noeleen.

'And wanking all over the place,' added Patricia, a woman of few, but frank, words. She set down her glass with an unsteady hand. Everyone knew she had a bit of a drink problem. God knows what she'd had in private before she'd tipped the Prosecco down on top of it. 'There's no sock or facecloth safe in my house from the filthy bastards.'

Silence, and then a burst of laughter.

'Jesus, Patricia, that's minging,' said Sonia. 'The wee dirtbags!'

'Don't be looking at me like that. Think yours'll be any better?' said Patricia, laughing. 'It comes to us all, no matter how carefully you raise them. There's not one woman at this table who won't be picking up a sock one day dried so stiff it'd cut your fingers off.'

The silence stretched just a moment too long.

'Shit. Sorry, Gemma. That came out wrong.'

They destroy your life …

'Ach sure, when you think about it, isn't it maybe just as well?'

'I don't think so actually, Mum.'

'Well, think about it from the outside, Gemma.' Joan leaned back in her armchair and waved her cigarette. Smoke trailed in a gentle spiral towards the yellowed ceiling.

'From the outside?'

'Yes, I mean try not to be so wrapped up in yerself.'

'Jesus! Thanks, Mum.'

'I'm serious. Children change a marriage – and not always for the best. Your dad and I were happy enough at the start.'

'I'm sorry, are you actually blaming us for the fact that you walked out and left us?'

'No, I'm not. I'm not blaming you – none of you. I love all my children equally.'

'Like fuck you do!'

'It's time to let that go.' Her mother sighed and dragged hard on the fag until the ash quivered and threatened to drop onto her lap.

It was no secret that Gemma's oldest brother, Rory, was the blue-eyed boy in his mother's eyes. Less than a year after he had fucked off to America, instead of staying to eventually inherit his father's farm, Joan had bolted.

'So we destroyed your marriage and ruined your life. Anything else you'd like to add?'

'There's no need for melodrama, Gemma. I've already said I don't blame my children for the fact that I married an absolute shit. But' – she stubbed out her fag after lighting another from its tip – 'but it did make a big impact later on. You know, I met Paddy a good ten years before I actually left yer da.'

'Yes, Mother. The whole fucking twenty townlands around knows that. And what a charming story it is. Sneaking around for ten years. D'you think I never knew before what a hindrance your kids were to your love life?'

'That's not nice. And it's not even true.' Joan sat up straighter and looked over at a large figure, slumped in an oversized armchair with a Laura Ashley loose cover. The man looked back, glanced at Gemma and turned away. Her mother's *fancy man*, the bogeyman of Gemma's teenage years: Paddy Buckley.

In the fourteen months since her father died, Gemma had given herself permission to come to her mother's home. For years before that they had met on neutral territory, if you could call a hotel or restaurant neutral territory. Paddy Buckley and Dominic McCann had been briefly under the same roof three times in all those years, sitting in separate pews as three of the McCanns' four children pronounced their marriage vows. As Gemma had walked up the aisle on her father's arm she had gripped him with a fierce, bruising intensity and felt the raging, seething power of the hard-muscled farmer who could have sent Buckley to hospital, or to the grave, with one well-aimed blow.

At her father's graveside fifteen years later, flanked by Cormac and Alo, Gemma had watched Buckley through lowered lashes as he threw up an invisible force field around her mother, deflecting all hint of criticism and sly looks and enveloping her in love.

Over the past year, in the fussy, matchy-matchy living room of Joan and Paddy's home, Gemma had started to relax and speak freely in a way she wouldn't have imagined possible before. Paddy would loll in his armchair, hands folded primly on the bulge of his enormous gut, giving him the serene appearance of a heavily pregnant woman. He would nod and smile, never interrupting or contradicting the woman he loved. When Joan left the room, however briefly, he seemed to shrink into himself, like a plant suddenly plunged into shadow, her return bringing the sun back from behind the clouds.

He would accept, with a smile and a squeeze of the hand, the laden side plate Joan offered him – apple tart or cream cakes, and a cup of tea – and balance the plate on the swelling rise of his gut – *nature's shelf*, he called it. It was all Gemma could do not to stare. Then she would imagine hoisting a belly of her own, the skin pulled taut, not over kilos of visceral fat but over the hard, struggling limbs of her unborn child. Sometimes she had to pull her eyes away from Paddy's belly to stare instead at the swan-necked Lladró figurines on her mother's mantelpiece and her collection of dumpy little Hummel children.

Gemma had expected her never-divorced mother to remarry as soon as Dominic died – to formalise a relationship now almost a quarter of a century old – but there was no sign of it. 'She'll be after her portion of the estate now,' whispered Alo to Cormac in the boneyard as the sexton dropped the green AstroTurf cover over Dominic's grave. But not only had Joan not contested the will, she had voluntarily signed away her legal entitlement, turning up with a copy of the document for each of her four children at Dominic's Month's Mind Mass.

Her mother spoke at last. 'I wish you would stop twisting my actions, Gemma. I stayed until you were almost in college. I could have left when you were nine years old. God knows, there were days I came close.'

'Sorry, Mum, it's just not an easy topic.'

'I know, but honestly, is it not time you stopped being so bloody touchy? Half the women in the world – and they all love their children, whether you believe it or not – would wave a magic wand if they could and go back to the way things were before. Look at you. You've a great life. Lots of women would envy you – plenty of money, a husband who thinks the sun shines out of your ass, free to live your life how you like, and come and go as you please.' Joan leaned in for the habitual last sentence in this recurrent conversation. 'After all ...'

Pause. Light. Stub. Drag. Exhale. Gemma waited, coiled like a spring, hoping her mother might have the sense to shut up for once.

'... after all, if you really wanted a child that badly you'd have adopted.'

'FUCK! Will you shut the fuck up? Why won't you all mind your own fucking business?' At Gemma's howl, the sleeping tabby leapt off the hearth rug and shot out through the cat flap in the patio door. 'I'm sick, sore and tired of this shit. Why won't you all leave me the fuck alone?'

Her mother sucked on her Silk Cut. Paddy shifted uneasily in his armchair. Gemma tried to control her breathing. Her mother tapped her cigarette on the edge of the brimming cut-glass ashtray.

The silence stretched out, much more than just a moment too long.

'Shit. Sorry, Mum. That came out wrong.'

Paddy Buckley hauled himself out of his chair and moved to the door. 'I'll wet the tay,' he said.

'Thanks, love.'

'Thanks, Paddy.'

On the patio, the cat stretched and turned, showing its pink belly to the last rays of the evening sun.

The Eighth

:::::

'God, the bloody Free Staters are at it again. Can they never leave anything well enough alone?'

'What are they at now? Is it NAMA or the banks or what?'

You might as well give up and let your visitor talk. Father Peter Matthews knows that you have as much interest in politics as the man in the moon, but he's rustling his newspaper and glaring at you over the rims of his reading glasses. There's no hope for it. A man who likes the sound of his own voice is Peter.

'Do you never pay any attention to the news?' he says.

'Even less than I used to. It's the same over and over. I'm old enough to just hope I'll be in the boneyard before Trump and Putin start the next bloody chapter.'

'Ah, would you give over about Trump. I told you it's the bloody Free Staters I'm talking about.' Peter sniffs and flaps the folded pages at you, as if the knowledge of their import will fly through the ether and lodge in your brain. 'And you're not much older than I am, for God's sake, sitting over there letting on to be Methuselah.'

'Well, we're both old enough to know who Methuselah is, and Melchisidech too, which is more than could be said about the handful of young lads below in the seminary.'

'Or any of those bloody wannabe lay deacons.'

You both sigh at that. What young single man in his right mind would become a lay deacon? No chance of a wife, a vow of chastity, parish accounts to muddle through, and not even a Roman collar to take the worst of the sting out of it? Someone who's running away from something, that's what you think.

Peter reaches the paper over to you and you grunt a little as you stretch forward to take it. He can say what he likes, but there's nothing like a soft chair in front of a fire to make you feel your age pressing down on your shoulders. Normally after Sunday lunch, you'd be slumped dozing in the ancient wingback chair that Peter has today claimed as his own. He has driven forty miles to help you fill the numb hours between Mass and devotions, and you're wishing you were asleep in your solitude, and resentful that he's stolen your chair. *What a miserable oul' fucker you are sometimes, Anthony.*

You scan the page. 'What is it I'm supposed to be looking at?' But your heart sinks when you spot it.

'Can't you see it? Down there at the bottom left? They're trying to repeal the eighth.'

'Repeal the eighth? What's that about?' *Why are you playing this game? He knows you aren't blind, deaf or dumb.*

'For fuck sake, Anthony, the eighth amendment to the Constitution. The anti-abortion amendment. The Left is looking for a repeal.'

'And then what? Another bloody referendum I suppose, and us

eejits stuck in the middle. Christ, the bishop'll be in his element, writing pastoral letters and expecting us to read them out to churches full of pensioners and little children. And the mothers'll be raging in the cars on the way back home, trying not to answer the children's questions. And the fathers'll say, *What do you expect?* and *I don't know why you bring the kids down there anyway and make them listen to those old paedos telling decent people how to live their lives.*'

'God, it's awful.' Peter looks at the fire and there's a shake in his voice. 'Here we are again, thirty years later, talking about the wholesale murder of Irish babies paid for by our taxes.'

'Well now, they're not exactly *our* taxes, are they, Peter? I mean, we're not in the same jurisdiction. And anyway, I didn't earn enough to pay any tax last year, even when you take the house and car as benefit-in-kind.'

You are doing your best to steer the conversation from murder to mammon and hoping Matthews will take the bait. A session bitching about money and the ingratitude of your ancient, well-pensioned parishioners is as much politics as you feel fit for today. You catch the eye of Our Lady, gently amused under her pale blue flowing headdress, a hijab by any other name, and you know that today your tactics won't work.

'Will you have a glass of wine, Peter? Or a whiskey?'

'At two o clock in the afternoon, and me with an hour's drive home? Will you have a titter of wit, man. Now what are we going to do about these repealers?'

You sit back in your chair, the less comfortable one, the brown leather slippery and treacherous. The chair is tolerable only when it is fully reclined, and although you have known Peter Matthews for forty years, you don't feel able to pull that lever and loll back while he talks to you about abortion and sin and the catechism. It is probably a good thing Peter has said no to the drop of drink – in the years since the confession of the prostitute-abusing-fiancé you and Pope Francis have been hitting the bottle a bit more often and with a heavier hand than before. *If you're not careful, Anthony, you'll be turning into a big alcoholic cliché.*

'I don't see that there's much we can do, Peter.'

You clasp your hands and concentrate on not picking at your cuticles, a filthy habit and your first recourse during times of stress. You have treated several throbbing hang-nail infections with the hot bread poultice that you learned from your mother on the farm, back when a body would want to be half-dead before seeing a doctor, but your old fingers heal a lot more slowly now.

'Well, couldn't we start a petition, or hold a march?' Peter leans forward in his chair – *your* chair – and his eyes are alight with the fervent glow of a much younger man. The last time you glimpsed such zeal in his eyes was back in 1979 when he was practising the new papal refrain *Totus Tuus, Totally Yours* with the junior choir for the big diocesan pilgrimage to see John Paul II in Drogheda.

'A march? You sound half-cracked, Peter.'

'Well, a Solemn Novena then. Nine weeks. A different speaker every week. We could put the feelers out, see how many parishes would join in. If we had enough, we could palm the organising off onto Sarah Reilly.'

There are no flies on Peter Matthews; he's as twisty as a bent corkscrew. If he can foist all the admin work onto the diocesan secretary, he'll get all the credit with none of the paperwork. *Bully for you, Matthews. Your ma didn't breed any fools.*

'Well, sure no one's stopping you. Ring around a few of the younger lads and see if anyone wants to join up.'

'So that's two parishes anyway. How many d'you think we'd need?'

You hold up a hand slowly and take a deep breath. It is time. You curse the bloody sleeveen government of the Republic of Ireland with its cowardice, prevarication and hypocrisy. You curse the repealers and their refusal to take no for an answer. You curse your past vigorous and vocal support of SPUC in the 1980s when you strutted around your parishes wearing two tiny silvered feet, the size of a little finger nail – the size of the feet of a twelve-week-old foetus – as a badge of honour, exhorting teenage girls fresh from that field in Drogheda, or the Phoenix Park, to join the Society for the Protection of the Unborn Child. Why the hell did Matthews have to ask this of you? What cursèd misfortune brought him and his newspaper here today?

'I think I'll give it a skip, Peter. I wouldn't be able for it, to tell you the truth.'

'Sure it'll be no big job for you. We'll let Sarah get the bit between her teeth and she'll run the whole thing like clockwork.'

'I just don't think I'm able for it.'

'Would you catch yourself on, Anthony. We're talking about standing up and introducing a speaker. Five minutes a night once a week. It's little enough you're being asked to do.'

Matthews must realise he's gone too far, or he's seen your cheeks redden, for he leans forward and smiles apologetically. 'Listen, it'll be wee buns. Sure, you won't have to accommodate them or anything. A cup of tea and a sandwich and they'll be on their way.'

The time has come. *Have some balls, Anthony, and tell the man the truth. It's the very least he deserves, this faithful old friend, who hasn't had an original thought since he left the seminary – nor had many while he was there neither.*

'Peter, listen. Now please don't be talking when you should be listening. I think I'll sit this one out. I'm not sure we're both on the same side of this argument.'

Matthews takes a quare gunk at you. You wish people would stop doing that. Have you become as strange as all that in recent years? Why do people keep looking at you like that?

'You can't be serious? You *cannot* be fucking serious, Anthony? You're *not sure* you're against abortion? Have you been at the communion wine? Or are you taking the piss?'

This is not going to end well. If you get out of this on speaking terms that's maybe the most you can hope for. *Fuck it, Anthony, maybe you should just say, Gotcha! Of course I'll join in. Sign me up, ya big simp.* Otherwise, you may never again have to grudge your old friend his comfy seat by your fireside, nor wash his dirty lunchtime dishes.

'I just don't think it's always as simple as we used to think – '

'Simple! For Christ sake, what could be more simple? *Before I formed you in the womb I knew you, before you were born I consecrated you.* For fuck's sake, Anthony, if that's too complicated how about *Thou shalt not kill?*'

'What about the children, Peter? What about the children born to a life of pain and suffering? What about the babies who used to die and we used to bury them and say a Mass for their souls, and now they don't die, but live for years, screaming and weeping, while the parents turn white-haired and stoop under the pain?'

'And who are you to decide what a life is worth?'

'And who are you to decide how a couple will spend their God-given years? How brothers and sisters will shoulder the burden when the parents are gone?'

'It's different after the child is born, Anthony. For the love of God, have some sense. Of course it's a terrible shock when the doctor first gives the news, but when the child is born, the love kicks in – it's nature.'

'Did you ever hear the old women, exhausted after rearing their brood of a dozen, say that the spinster's child is easily reared? You could say the same for the bachelor, especially for a bachelor with the Roman collar. What would you know about how it feels to rear a child, healthy or otherwise? You've never wiped an arse other than your own, drip-dropped your hard-won breast milk through a tiny PEG stoma, nor stripped a soiled bed in the middle of the night when every sinew in your body is crying out for rest.'

'And you have?'

'I haven't, Peter – don't be fucking stupid – but there's a thing called the internet, and there's a thing called support groups, and there's a thing called reading and learning and not parroting the party line, especially when that party consists of smug old men who are lifted and laid, waited on hand and foot.'

'Are you talking about the cardinals? The representatives of Christ on earth?'

'You know fine well and rightly who I'm talking about. I'm talking about the men who said *to hell with transubstantiation, I'm sure we can let that one slide,* and welcomed the married Anglican clergy, and their offspring and their inheritance issues, into the Catholic priesthood, but who are asking our young men to throw themselves onto the crucifix of celibacy when we know what a fucking mess it makes of them. I'm talking about the people who'd ordain a married Protestant man rather than a Catholic nun, who has given her whole life to the service of God and man but has done it without the benefit of a penis.'

And there, your ungovernable rebellious tongue has done it again. If there had been any chance of salvage it is gone.

Matthews hauls himself up. You look at the dent his big ass has left in the threadbare fabric of your favourite chair, the chair you would have yielded to no one but him. Is this perhaps the last time a friend will sit here with you? Is this the final scene already, unbeknownst to you both? Will it be just you and the television, alone for the rest of your days?

'I'm leaving, Anthony. Thank you for the lunch. I'd lay a pound to a penny you're sickening for something and don't know it yet. Get yourself into bed. If you feel a fever or a weakness, for God's sake call the South West Doc service, and if they won't come, call 999.'

Matthews is a good, solid, unimaginative man, and a friend. *Stretch out your hand, Anthony. Use the small bit of wit you were born with and grab the lifebelt of Peter's excuse. Phone him tomorrow with a tale of food poisoning, and ask him to tell Sarah Reilly to organise your Solemn Novena.*

Matthews picks up his keys and pauses with his hand on the door. 'Go on to bed, Anthony. It's a twenty-four hour bug. These dismal imaginings will be just a distant memory when you're back at yourself again.'

You open your mouth. You open your mouth to say, *I will. Good man, I'll do that. I'll fix myself a hot-water jar and I'll have a lie down.*

'Peter,' you say, 'you're a teetotal fool and my best friend. I'll tell you the truth.' The words are flowing into you from outside your body and you vomit them out despite yourself. 'If men could get pregnant, abortion would be the eighth sacrament of the Catholic Church, and there'd be no talk of repeal.'

::::::

The slow, deliberate crunch of tyres on gravel carries away not your oldest friend, but certainly your most attentive. How long will it be, if ever, before those tyres crunch back in the opposite direction?

You sit in silence as the February gloom gathers around you. You glance up at Our Lady and wonder what *she* thinks, deep in her mysterious female heart. When Gabriel descended from out of the heavens and spake unto her, did she say, as we have always been told, 'Behold the handmaid of the Lord, be it done unto me according to thy will'? Or did she say, 'And be stoned to death as a pregnant unmarried whore? You must be fucking joking if you think I'm falling for that'?

This East Wind

::::

'Gemma, love. Are you busy this afternoon?'

'There's nothing outstanding until evening milking, Alo. Nothing that can't wait till tomorrow. Why? Is it a trip to the doctor?'

I watch the fear flash in her eyes. I'm well into my ninth decade now, but I'm not sure Gemma knows my full age. She glances at the backs of my hands where the dark purple warfarin splotches expand almost weekly – they've reached the second knuckles of the fingers now – until she catches my eye and looks away.

'No, love, I feel grand. I'll leave the quack-bothering for another day. Just wondering if you had an hour or two.'

She nods and smiles but she's confused. She drops me to the mart every Thursday, where I eat a roast beef dinner with Iggy and Sean and the other oul' men. She can't understand how we can bear to eat, the smell of the gravy mingling with the dung reeking off our boots under the table. That's cause her own da, thon miserable bastard, never brought her to the mart when she was young, or anywhere else, overlooking the cream of his crop, because she was a girl. Me and Iggy and Sean were raised during rationing, and we never pass up a meal. Iggy, in particular, would eat the hind leg off the lamb of Jesus.

Gemma drives me to the clubhouse when Drumaleish has a big match or to the county grounds when Tyrone are playing. But she doesn't bring me much anywhere else now – except Mass and funerals, and most of the old crowd are already under the ground.

Of all the indignities of old age, I feel the loss of the car the most. I've aged ten years since my heart attack last May. Gemma fusses over me like an oul' doll, till I'm totally scundered. She'll hardly even let me into the cab of the tractor, not since Mick Malone stepped awkwardly down out of his grandson's Fendt and wrecked himself. The shattered shin bone came right through his trouser leg; he's never left the hospital since. But my body and my mind are sound, thank God, and I want to go where I want to go before it's too late. I want to go today.

'I'll take you on a mystery tour, if I can find it …' I tell her.

I nearly take the hanger off the ceiling of the jeep as I haul myself up into the big passenger seat. It's a right job, all leather and chrome and as comfortable as an armchair.

Gemma whips out her phone. 'Where are we off to then?'

'No, no. I don't want to use the satnav. I want to take us there.'

'If I knew where *there* was,' she says.

'Drive on, daughter dear. I'm pretty sure of myself.'

There's a bit of cursing alright, a bit of stopping and thinking and holding the map up to the car window to catch the light. One time we have to do a three-point turn, and Gemma sighs and rolls her eyes when I give out about the bleepers and bells and reversing camera. They'd drive a body to drink, and hadn't millions of us managed our vehicles very well, thank you, without them.

'Stop. Stop. We're gone past it!'

'Fuck sake, Alo. Gone past what? I saw nothing.'

'No, I have it now. We're set. Turn her round again and turn on yer hazards. Slow as you like.'

'There's a van up my ass.'

'I'm uneasy about him! He can wait.'

And in fairness to him he did wait.

'Turn right, turn right. There it is, the car park.'

'It's a field, Alo.'

'No, it's the spot. X marks the spot. I toul' you we didn't need yer oul' Google Maps.'

Gemma heaves the jeep round in a right angle and pulls into a secluded, almost invisible, car park on a country road a few miles from Stewartstown.

Tullyhogue Fort.

Of course I know it means climbing up a hill – I mean, a fort is bound to be on a hill. But Jesus Christ! I feel my heart hammering agin my breastbone as I pant, wheeze and struggle up a slippery grass path. I've brought the ashplant – I'd never get up without it, digging it deep into the wet soil and levering myself forward one pace at a time. About ten years ago Gemma bought me an oul' fella's walking stick with a smooth machine-wrought handle and a rubber knob on the end, but I wouldn't be seen dead using thon.

Gemma follows me over the ruts and clabber, cursing softly as the wet soaks through her gutties and she sinks into the mud. (Why she doesn't stick to the leather ankle boots is beyond me.) At the top of the path, a complex series of bars, lashed and bolted to a galvanised mobile cattle crush, blocks the way. A dozen whitehead bullocks don't bother to rise to greet us; they just carry on chewing the cud and licking the snotters from their nostrils. A fine bunch of beasts – any other day I'd have stopped to take a look – but today I'm focused on the barrier in the path.

'Hell's curse it,' I say and half-collapse on the top rail, blowing like a broken-winded oul' horse. 'This is a public right of way – sacred land. They've no right to close it off like this.'

The crush is six foot high, rusted into place, metal bars slippery with algae. A recipe for a broken fibula in another oul' eejit.

'Never mind,' I say. 'We tried. We may as well go home.'

Gemma sighs. 'Don't be such an almighty drama queen, Alo.' She wanders off to the right.

I grip the top bar with every ounce I have left and struggle over the high metal structure. As my boots hit the ground on the other side, I land at Gemma's feet.

'No fool like an old fool,' she mutters, pointing at the accessible pedestrian gate twenty yards away.

I've given my knees and hips a right bloody jar, landing down off the fence, but not many men of my age would even have tried it, so I bite my lip and limp over to a gap between the outer earthwork walls and into the ceremonial mound.

'Tullyhogue Fort means *the mound of the young warriors*,' Gemma reads out from the illustrated noticeboard.

'I know that. What do you take me for?'

'*It is a large mound, or man-made hill, with a depressed centre, surrounded by stately two-hundred-year-old trees. It is an ancient ceremonial site where the chieftains of Tyrone (Tír Eoghain, the land of Eoghan), were crowned.*'

'Gemma, pet, for the love of God, would you please pack it in?'

She continues to read the noticeboard in silence, face on her like a slapped arse, but I'm so old now I can get away with a bit of gratuitous rudeness.

I should have brought Sean O'Neill with me, although him and Gemma rub each other up the wrong way on account of him being the most genial, casual fuckin' bigot left walking the land since they planted Paisley. Sean would have got a kick out of standing on this site, pontificating, and seeing in his mind's eye the kneeling form of O'Hagan, the sept and hereditary protector of Tullyhogue Fort, placing the ceremonial golden sandal on the foot of the newly crowned Earl. The O'Neill, *the proudest title in Ulster Gaeldom*, says Sean. Sean is always gurnin' on about his lineage, leading directly back to Eoghan, son of King Niall of the Nine Hostages, *lost in the mist of Celtic mythology,* which is not so easy to say at Sean's age after a few pints and the dentures far too big for his shrunken gums.

'What's this rock called again, Alo?'

Gemma kicks at some slumped, smashed lumps of stone and I wince.

The *Leac na Rí* lies in pieces at our feet, shattered and tumbled by Lord Mountjoy during the Nine Years' War when the first Elizabeth was on the throne. A mean and bitter end for the Stone of the Kings. I close my eyes and try to shut out the scene of Mountjoy and his men laying into the ceremonial stone throne made of three large slabs placed around the *Leac na Rí*. I can hear the ringing of the blows, sledgehammer and mace upon granite, and the tortured creaking as the slabs give way, yielding the sacred Stone to the pillaging soldiers. Or perhaps it's my own pulse that sings in my ears as the oul' heart strives to recover from the long uphill trek.

'Gemma, do you know nothing? It's Ulster's *Lia Fáil*, our Stone of Destiny, sacred symbol of the Gaelic way of life, of Brehon law passed down through the annals of the Four Masters, to be administered by Gaelic judges.'

'Have you been at Google again?'

I didn't even dignify that with a response. 'The last physical remnant of the supremacy of the clans. Our *Leac na Rí* is far older and more sacred than the Stone of Scone, which them English bastards stole and built into the coronation chair of Edward Longshanks, as if that would give them fuckers legitimacy for stealing Scotland too.'

'Well, at least they didn't smash that one.'

'At least they've sent it back to Edinburgh at long last. It's sitting there, waiting to be returned to Westminster Abbey when that oul' bitch in Buckingham Palace finally pops her clogs.'

'The Scots had a referendum, Alo, and the separatists lost. Maybe it's time to start thinking more about the future and less about the Battle of Bannockburn.'

'You think? We'll see what Brexit has to say about that.'

'So the Stone was destroyed in the Nine Years' War,' says Gemma. 'Which one was that, again?'

'Only the final battle for the heart and soul of Ulster. The one that sparked the Flight of the Wild Geese. Did you learn nothing at school?'

'I did do a little bit about Tullyhogue in history. In fact, we came out here on a field trip when I was in First Year. All I remember is that we got to wear our own clothes instead of the bloody school uniform. History in school was mostly Celts and Normans, Strongbow and Aoife. They weren't too big on teaching Ulster plantation history slap bang in the middle of the Troubles. Afraid to turn us all into raging Provos probably.'

I decide to stop listening to her oul' nonsense, so I gaze at the wide expanse of countryside. The hills on the horizon glimmer in the far distance. Strategically, you couldn't beat Tullyhogue. I turn from side to side, the full circle. No way you could approach this place by stealth. Any marching body of men would be spotted miles away by the watchful O'Hagans.

The wind flares up and licks at the corners of my eyes, which I've been having fierce trouble with since the cataract operations. I'm supposed to wear sunglasses, but I feel a right stumer in them.

'I've waited such a long time to come here,' I say finally, breaking the wind-whipped silence between us. How can I stay angry at Gemma? 'You know, I've never been here before in my life.'

'What? Why not? Sure you'd be here in forty minutes if you didn't keep taking the wrong road.'

'I was born in nineteen and thirty-five. In school in them days, the only field trip you did was if that carn Master Dillon made you go out into the field and cut your own sally rod to get beat with.' I rub my eye again; the wind was after blowing dust into it. 'Then, when Bid was alive, I was far too busy making money to think about day trips, unless it was to the ploughing or a livestock show. Then, when she was dead, I was far too busy guarding Cormac to have time for gadding around the country.'

'I still don't understand why you never came here before, and you so keen on your history,' says Gemma. 'Surely you could have found a few hours.'

'I heard tell you could stand on Tullyhogue Hill and look out over the landscape of *Tír Eoghain*, at the land of Eoghan Roe, and Hugh Roe and Phelim O'Neill, but that after the Troubles came all you could see was them hills in the distance littered with British Army spy posts, and listening towers bristling with radar and satellite dishes. Instead of the wind in the trees you'd hear the army fly their shit-ooks over the hill of The O'Neill on their way to the helipads in Dungannon or Omagh. I couldn't bear to stand at the site of the *Leac na Rí* and see the blight on the landscape.'

Silence hangs around us. I look about me and draw the clean fresh air of Ireland into my lungs. For sure and certain, this will be my one and only trip to Tullyhogue. Maybe my last trip anywhere.

It's the end of the line for the family. My brother Anthony says he's getting planted into the big plot with me and Bid, which is unusual, but he's been alone all his life and dreads the ostentatious solitude of a priest's grave.

I won't live to see my heir's heir, since Gemma and Cormac told me to quit moithering them; that adoption was my dream, not theirs. When they're lowered down on top of the three of us oul' ones, that'll be the end of the O'Donovans.

But at least I lived long enough to see the British Army sent back home, and to see thon other bunch of useless, throughother eejits installed at Stormont, for all the good that does us. The politicians haven't done a hand's turn for nigh on two years now, bickering about budget cuts, and cash-for-ash, and street signs in the Irish language, but it's a damn sight better than everyone trying to blow each other to kingdom come in the alleyways of Belfast and the quiet pubs of country villages.

Gemma hands me a tissue, one of those useless wee folded up ones out of a packet that women seem to always have about them and that fall apart after one good blow.

'Well, the army have gone now, Alo.'

'Aye, they're gone now. Thanks be to God. Eoghan Roe, and Hugh and the rest of the O'Neills can rest easy in their graves at last. And I can die happy.'

After a moment, she puts her hand on my arm and gently dabs at my cheeks as if I'm crying. As if I'm a wee child crying. The barefaced cheek of her.

'Damn it to hell and back, we'll go home now, love,' I say. 'This east wind is cuttin' the eyes out of me.'

Glossary

:::::

acting the lig: acting the fool

as rich as creosote: creosote is used to preserve fencing timbers. This phrase is a farmer's play on the phrase *'as rich as Croesus'*

amadán: a stupid or foolish man

banbh: piglet

boke, to boke: vomit

blirt: a derogatory term, a generic insult

brew: on the brew, unemployment payment; derives from bureau (unemployment bureau)

buachaillain buí: ragwort (a poisonous, notifiable weed)

carn: an unpleasant, despised person; derives from wood-kerne (an outlaw)

clabber: deep mud or muck (from the Irish clábar)

cleg: a biting horse-fly

cowp: to tip or knock something over

dunt: a gentle prod with foot, head, elbow, shoulder

geansaí: jumper or sweater

geg: a gag, a joke, a joker

glipe: a fool, a messer

gom: an idiot or useless person

guldering: aggressive shouting

gurning: complaining, moaning, repetitive talk

gutties: running shoes, trainers

hot press: airing cupboard

jouk: a feint in sport, a quick, deceptive movement

juke: a quick glance

latchiko: a fool, a messer

lock: an indeterminate number, e.g. *a lock of sweets*

messages: groceries, errands

minging: filthy, disgusting

moily cow: a moiled/moily cow is from a breed that has no horns ('*it would freeze the horns off a moily cow*' equates to '*it would freeze the balls off a brass monkey*')

quare: queer, odd; e.g. *a quare gunk*, an odd look. Can be used as very, extremely, e.g. quare *and tight*

redding out: cleaning or emptying out; can also be *redding up*

scundered: fed up, frustrated; also embarrassed

Shit-ooks: a derogatory term for the British Army's Chinook helicopters

slabber: a person who does not know when to shut up; also *slabbering on*: talking too much

sleeveen: untrustworthy or cunning

stook: a bunch of harvested grain or grass

stumer: a stupid person

the day: today

thole: tolerate, bear

thon: those, that (derives from *that one, those ones*)

throughother: careless, lazy, feckless

Acknowledgements

Thanks are due to Libraries NI for their generous support for *The Accidental Wife*, in particular for choosing it as the Armagh Big Read of 2017 and for recommending it for the BBC Radio Ulster Nolan Show Book Club Choice, July 2017. Without their wonderful support in introducing my debut work to a vast number of readers, this new companion volume, *Full of Grace*, may never have been written.

To John MacKenna for his kind words on the cover.

To the John O'Connor Writing School and Literary Festival, Armagh, for support and encouragement.

To Greywood Arts Centre, Killeagh, Co. Cork, for peace and solitude, as the recipient of their inaugural Winter Writers' Retreat bursary.

To Alex Reece Abbott for constant moral support and practical guidance.

To Averill Buchanan for her keen editorial eye.

To Patricia Reilly and Sharon Walsh for proofreading.

To all my friends and writing colleagues in WomenAloudNI for their help and support.

To Debra Leigh Scott of Sowilo Press, Philadelphia, for kind permission to include 'Breathing' and 'The Visit', which were previously published in *The Accidental Wife* and which add so much to the narrative flow of *Full of Grace*.

To three wonderful independent local bookshops that have done much to support and promote my writing practice: Farrell and Nephew, Newbridge; Woodbine Books, Kilcullen; Barker and Jones, Naas.

To the members of the Rick O'Shea Book Club, who have done so much, by enthusiastic word-of-mouth, to share my work with new readers.

To Eimear O'Callaghan whose wonderful memoir *Belfast Days: a 1972 Teenage Diary* helped me, at last, to find a structure to tackle writing about the year of my birth.

To John Moriarty who was the first to bring my work to the attention of my wonderful publishers, Red Stag Books, and without whom we may never have met.

To my very patient children who live on crisp sandwiches when deadlines are pressing.

To my husband, Patrick, who refuses to let me quit.

To every reader who has contacted me to say: 'I never saw that word written down before,' or 'I haven't heard that phrase since my mother died' I say a special thank you. You are the reason I keep writing. You are the spur to my recording of the voices that are disappearing from our marts and schoolyards, our post offices and our rural communities. Thank you.

An Interview with Orla McAlinden

:::::

Q: Congratulations on the publication of *Full of Grace*, your third book and your second short story collection. After the success of your novel *The Flight of the Wren*, what prompted you to return to the short story form?

Orla: I have always loved the short story form. Visitors to my home are often taken aback when I show them shelf after shelf of short story collections. The received wisdom is that stories are impossible to sell and almost impossible to publish, but there are many niche publishers in Ireland specialising in the short story. I think the form lends itself to powerful subjects. I like to think of the short story as a swift punch in the gut, utterly surprising and completely unforgettable!

Q: And is it because you are looking for that 'punch in the gut' that you set your stories in Northern Ireland? Your novel was set in Kildare where you've lived for nearly twenty years, so what brings you back to the North when you write short fiction? Is it the potential for violence?

Orla: No. Not at all. Firstly, I think a good writer can get a powerful, gripping and intense story out of a trip to Tesco or from a family eating dinner in their own kitchen. Secondly, very few of my stories contain any explicit violence. Life in the countryside was very different during the Troubles. I find a lot of literature set in and around the Troubles period is very urban-centric, as if everyone lived in Belfast or Derry. I couldn't write a novel like Anna Burns' magnificent *Milkman* because I've no experience of the claustrophobia and isolation of people confined to just a few streets, afraid of the anonymous 'other'. In the country and the smaller towns, that sense of anonymity didn't exist.

Q: So why do you choose Northern Ireland as a setting?

Orla: Actually, I write about the North almost entirely because I am in love with the rural dialect. When I was a child I spent a lot of time with men, farmers mainly, and they made absolutely no allowances for my tender years! I was submerged in a vibrant, rich dialect that probably hadn't changed much for several hundred years. In many cases the rhythms of the sentences are Irish, grammatically speaking, translated directly into English. Phrases such as *throughother* and *hallion* and *hell's curse it* were still in common use during the 1970s and 80s. The smallest mistake or misunderstanding could result in a hail of insults and invective; an adult would never speak to a child that way now. After my father died, I decided to jot down a few of his favourite sayings, particularly his extensive and inventive repertoire of insults. People didn't curse quite as freely then as they do now, so for maximum impact you had to choose your insult carefully. It was in this memorial-writing process that I realised how impoverished my own language had become, how banal and homogenised the language my own children speak. My children's speech has more in common with Peppa Pig than with the glorious full throttle dialect I grew up with. So I looked around for books to read, to reconnect me with my childhood and to remind me of my dad's way of speech and that of his friends. I couldn't find many. There was Benedict Kiely, of course, Sam McAughtry, Sam Hanna Bell, but when I looked for contemporary works, I couldn't find them.

Q: There's an old cliché that a writer should write the book they want to read …

Orla: Definitely. That is precisely what I did. But I never really imagined anyone else would want to read it. For the first few years I wrote entirely for my own amusement.

Q: And now you write for a living.

Orla: God, no. I am very definitely a hobbyist. It took me two years to find a publisher for *The Accidental Wife*, and that turned out to be a small American press. It took four years to find a publisher brave enough to take on the novel; nobody wanted to release a book about prostitution during the famine! I don't write for a living, and if I did, I don't think I'd have the freedom to write what I care most about. Publishing and writing is a business; if you want to eat, you need a good commercial brain. I don't worry too much about the commercial potential of my books. I know that if I look hard enough for long enough, I will eventually find a publisher prepared to take a risk. Luckily for me at this time, that's Red Stag – they love the work and they're prepared to support a relatively unknown writer like me.

Q: Can we expect more northern stories in the future then?

Orla: I'm sure more will come in time, but the book I am working on now is another historical novel, and it happens to be set in Tipperary about the turn of the last century – 1895 to be precise.

Q: Can you tell us more, or is it a deathly secret?

Orla: Not at all. It's a novel about the death by burning of Bridget Cleary, ostensibly because her husband felt she had been possessed by fairies. I'm far from the first writer to explore this well-known story, but I hope I can bring something new to it.

Q: It couldn't be more different!

Orla: True, but I started it when I was writing *The Flight of the Wren*, which is set in 1849, so it didn't feel like such a big leap at the time. I've included a sample chapter of the new novel here to whet readers' appetites.

Q: I look forward to that.

Orla: Me too. This may sound like a strange thing to say about a historical novel about real, well-documented people and events, but I have no idea what's going to happen in the new novel. I don't plot or plan, I just let the story come. I can't wait to see what happens.

Preview of work in progress: *The Fairy Woman*

This is an extract from the opening pages of the first draft of a new novel, *The Fairy Woman*, about the life and tragic death of Brigid Cleary. You can keep up to date with the progress of this novel, and other works by Orla McAlinden at www.orlamcalinden.com and www.flightofthewren.com.

The White Hare

:::::

It was a dispute over butter churns that first brought Bridget to Josie's door. Where Josie was short and redhaired, with the shocking white skin and invisible brows and lashes of the red head, Bridget was tall and dark, and striking enough to stop a carriage on the road. In truth she was a beautiful woman.

'Step in, girl, don't fear.'

Bridget opened the lower half of the door and stepped into the dusk. While her eyes adjusted to the dim half-light, Josie sat back in the shadow of the inglenook and took a long appraising look. Her visitor's apron was flat and tight across her waist, no sign of swelling, or thickening, no hint of the pregnancy that she and her husband must surely be starting to fear would never happen.

'Mistress Boylan —'

'My name is Josie. And you are Bridget Cleary who was Boland.'

Bridget nodded her head, but didn't look surprised. It wouldn't take the skills of a wise woman to know her name. She was the best looking woman for twenty townlands around and was known the length and breadth of them as a seller of eggs on monthly account and a dressmaker of great skill.

'Will you sit?'

Bridget gathered her skirts around her and sat a respectful distance from the warmth of the fire and folded her hands in her lap. She remained silent, head bowed, and waited for the older woman to speak.

'I've been expecting you. I am not surprised to see you.' And Josie wasn't surprised. She had not known, as she heard the subtle change in the soundscape of the hill, exactly who was toiling upwards to her cottage, but she had been expecting this woman for years. A woman who marries at barely eighteen years old, and who marries the most sullen, dark-spirited man in the county, when she has the beauty and the liberty of youth to pick and choose, must have a story worth telling. And if that story is not the usual story of a rapidly filling womb, as time had proven it not to be, then it is a story that sooner or later will need to be laid at the feet of a wise woman.

'What will you ask me, in return for your help?' Bridget said.

'Well, that's not a pretty greeting.' Josie sighed, and gestured towards the bunches of drying herbs and the pestle, mortars and close-stoppered bottles which stood to attention on the old dresser beside the table. 'Do you think these secret herbs walked in here, off the mountain, cleaned themselves and said the sacred incantations over themselves? Do you think I should work for charity, until I starve to death and take all my learning and lore into the boneyard with me? That'd be no good service to the people round here.'

Bridget muttered a quiet apology and fixed a wayward strand of hair behind her ear. She wore the long, hooded cloak of the married woman, and her blue eyes shone out with shocking intensity from inside the folds of black cloth. At length she reached up and pulled the hood back onto her shoulders. A sharply delineated red mark coloured the whole of her left cheek.

'I can see the fingermarks from here,' Josie said. 'He's after catching you a fine wallop, but don't worry, your beauty won't be marred for long, it was only an open-handed slap I'd say.' She rose from her chair and examined the mark with interest. 'And does he hit you often?'

'It wasn't my husband.'

'Oho, was it not? Who else but a husband strikes a married woman? Unless it was the priest? I'm having nothing to do with cursing a priest.'

Bridget raised her hand to her face and gently traced the contours of the mark. 'It was Susan Egan who done it. She has had no butter come good since the last time I was on her yard. I went last Friday to collect the money she owes me for the eggs. She's useless with hens, can't keep them alive above a fortnight, so she gets her eggs from me.'

'And now her butter won't churn.'

'That's right. She was a shilling short and I had words with her. She gave me a shove – you know what a temper she has on her.' Josie nodded. 'I went reeling backwards, caught my hand on the dash of the churn to stop my fall. Now her milk won't churn and she's blackguarding me and calling my name out below in the village as a fairy, or worse. When I told her to stop, she drew back and slapped me. In public.'

'And why is it that your own mother won't help you break the hex and defend you?'

Bridget dropped her gaze for a moment as a fine blush crept out of the collar of her dress and spread up her throat. 'Mistress Boylan, I think you know as well as I do, that my mother is no more a wise woman than the man in the moon. She never claims to be a wise woman. She has deft, tiny hands that are useful for the birthing of tangled twin lambs and over-big calves, and she has a quiet calm mind to work out what way the animal is lying within the womb, and how's best to proceed. And that's all her prowess. If the people around here call her a fairy-taught midwife, well maybe she ought to stop them, but she never encourages them, and as you know, she never, ever lays hands on a human woman.'

'That's true. She knows her limits. So your mother won't help you?'

'No, she's staying well out of it. And the Egans are after getting Denis Ganey from the foothills of Slievenamon, and he has fixed the butter with a charm, and bid them ban me from the yard and house for evermore.' Her voice shook and dropped in tone. 'I'm after losing a customer who took two dozen eggs a month, I'll never see the shilling she owes me, and Ganey has people convinced I hexed the churn.'

'What do you want me to do? I won't meddle where Ganey has already been. You can't get two cunning-folk mixed up in the same hex, especially not when one of them is a slieveen, and is hand-in-glove with the fairies of the mountain. God knows where it would end.'

Bridget raised her head at last and stared straight in Josie's eyes. 'Do you believe him, then? Do you believe I put the bind on the churn? Susan said she dashed it for three hours, until her arms were shaking and she even asked her husband to try too, without so much as a lump of butter starting. After Ganey had said his charm and added not even a half ounce of his own specially blessed butter, within three strokes, the whole churn dashed properly.'

Josie sighed. 'I don't think you cursed the churn, Bridget. I don't think you even know how. You're right about your mother, she has skills but no knowledge and no gift. How could she have passed onto you what she never had herself?'

'What then? What would have happened? Can't you give me an explanation that I can take to the Egans before they blacken my name even further?'

Josie paused for a moment, scooping a fingerful of salve out of a small earthenware pot and rubbing it gently onto the already fading mark on her visitor's face. It was no harm to be seen to help along those ailments that, if left alone, she knew would cure themselves. She paused with her hand still on the young woman's shoulder.

'I can't go against Ganey. I can't say the churn wasn't cursed when he has already proved that it was and has broken the curse. But I can undo the slander against you. I know what has happened. I should have told John and Susan Egan what I saw last week, but it slipped my mind.'

Bridget was leaning forward in her seat, breathing fast. 'What did you see? Did you see something that will clear my name?'

'I did. Just last week, I saw a white hare in the Egan haggard, where the two cows were cudding. It was just before the dawn, when I was gathering necessities for the drenches I made for Peter Murphy's goat. It was so dark I wouldn't have seen the hare, but for it was a ghostly white colour, and it shimmered in the first gloaming.'

'A white hare?' Bridget whispered.

'A white hare, with the teat of Egan's moiled cow in its mouth, sucking away.'

'A fairy?'

'Of course a fairy. That's where the curse came from that Ganey has lifted.'

'What will I do?'

'Do nothing. I'll see John Egan myself, and Susan, and I'll clear your name. They'll be glad to know it wasn't a neighbour who would curse them and wish them ill.'

'And what will I pay you?'

Josie waved her hand, and shook her head graciously. 'Ach, Bridget love, don't mention it. I'm doing nothing, only telling what I should have thought to tell before. It hasn't cost me any of my skill, or sucked any of the strength from me, for Ganey has taken the risk and the fairy-fury onto himself. There's no payment needed.'

But you will pay, Josie thought, as her visitor gabbled thanks, and blessings, offered her a half dozen chances to change her mind about payment, then finally gathered back up her hood and re-tied the strings of the cloak for the walk back down the steep hill-path.

You will pay, when you think to come back to me for the potions that will catch a child's soul and keep it in your belly for the nine months that's needed. Oh yes, Miss high-and-mighty Cleary, with your egg money and your Singer sewing machine, and your customers coming from as far as Tipperary Town for the hats you make. A little bit of that income will be coming my way soon enough, for every man wants an heir, and five years is a long, long time to wait.